8123

An Unfinished War

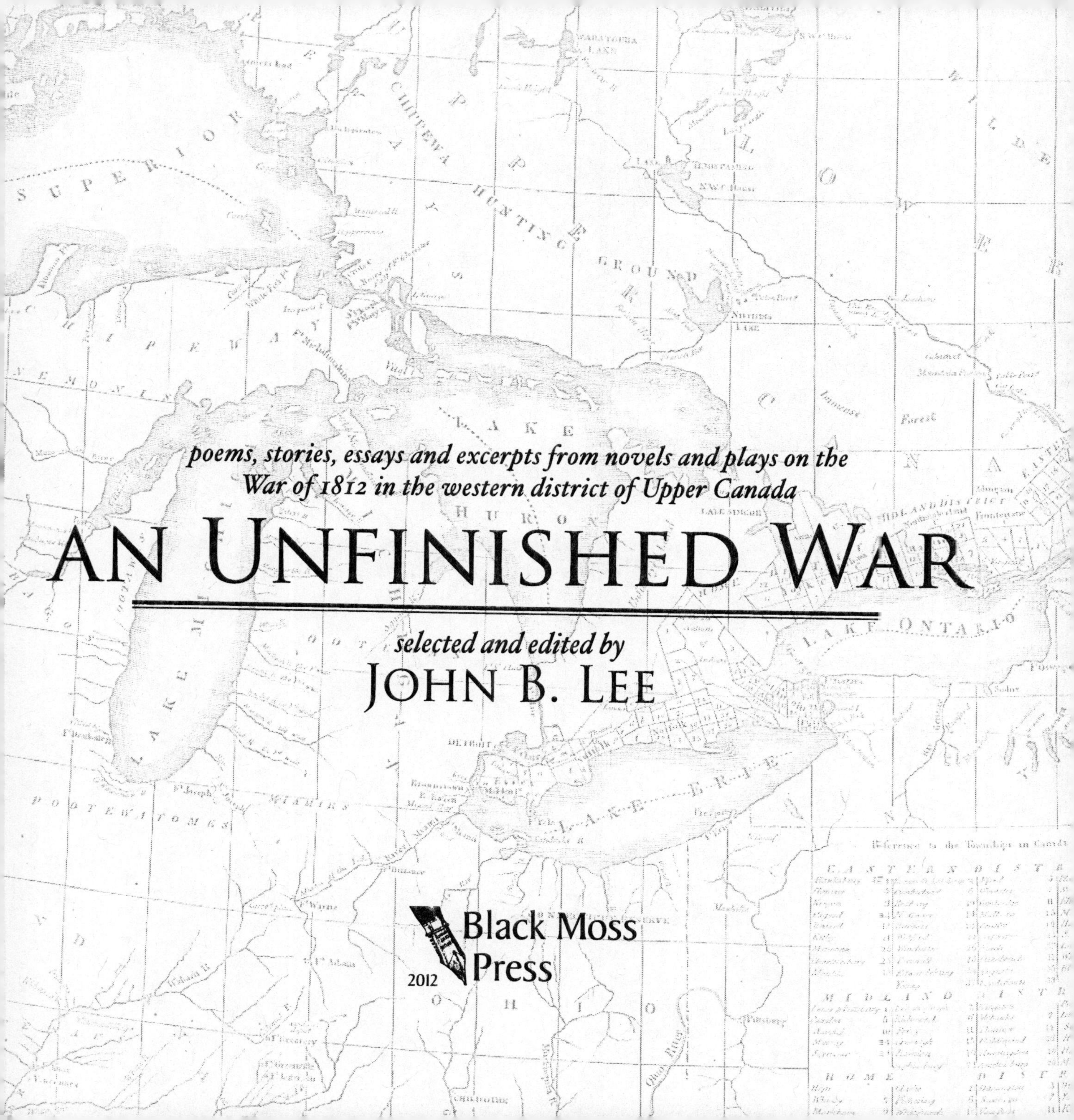

poems, stories, essays and excerpts from novels and plays on the War of 1812 in the western district of Upper Canada

AN UNFINISHED WAR

selected and edited by

JOHN B. LEE

Black Moss Press
2012

"Most of the people have lost all confidence.
I however speak loud and look big!"
British General Isaac Brock, June 1812

"The acquisition of Canada this year, as far as the neighborhood
of Quebec, will be a mere matter of marching..."
Thomas Jefferson in a letter to William Duane, August 1812

"Send them back whence the whites came. Back to the great water whose
accursed waves brought them to our shores. War now.
War always. War on the living. War on the dead."
Tecumseh

"One is formed to rule; another to obey."
from a sermon by the Reverend John Strachan of York

"I am flattered at being ranked among the enemies of the King's servants in this Colony, I glory in the distinction."
Joseph Willcocks, The Upper Canadian Guardian, June 9, 1812

"What in the name of heaven can be done with such a vile population?"
General Isaac Brock in a statement lamenting the disaffection of the populace in Upper Canada

Cataloguing information can be obtained through Library and Archives Canada Cataloguing in Publication

ISBN 978-0-88753-511-6

Cover photo:
Battle of Queenston Heights, James B. Dennis (Library and Archives Canada, public domain)

Interior Map:
To the officers of the Army and the citizens of the United States, this map of Upper and Lower Canada and United States contigious Contracted from the Manuscript surveys of P. F. Tardieu Is respectfully inscribed by the publicks most Obedient Servant Thomas Kensett (Thomas Kensett, 1812, public domain)

Layout & design:
Kate Hargreaves

Published by Black Moss Press at 2450 Byng Road, Windsor, Ontario, N8W 3E8 Canada. Black Moss books are distributed in Canada and the U.S. by LitDistCo. All orders should be directed there.

Black Moss Press
EST. 1969

Black Moss Press books can also be found on our website www.blackmosspress.com.

Black Moss would like to acknowledge the generous financial support from both the Canada Council of the Arts and the Ontario Arts Council.

PRINTED IN CANADA

contents

1813

1814

1815-16

present day

I sit in the parking lot...

John B. Lee

I sit in the parking lot of the Legion in Fort Erie, Ontario. Here, the world that was is paved over, hemmed in, lost in the rig-drone of the city under the long grey shadow of the Peace Bridge connecting Canada to industrial Buffalo. The green Niagara seems but a slow thought flowing by. I've come to contemplate a death, unmourned. Unfound bones. Somewhere beneath me, in among the multitude of anonymous dead, lie the non-shriven remains of one who fell so long ago he's dust, and what's left of the body and the weird half-skull shape of what it meant to be a man. And what I feel is the great disappointment of absent ghosts. The busy indifference of truckers and tourists. Amnesia of asphalt, black and smelling of tar, impervious to light, opaque and unforgiving. Here I sit, where the veterans of the last great war come to remember and forget, to revere and regret, to honour heroes and grieve the dead, to say of their fellows, "I knew him once, he was my friend," and to weep at the thought of him gone, and to laugh for the days spent together when they were all young.

I try to think of the rain and smoke and heat and long-ago noise of a different battle. I try to think, here, on this very ground, was the British battery set to lay siege on old Fort Erie, 800 yards away. One man leading a smallish band of men came in wet September, proud in his officer's uniform, brave in his mission, setting a picket to keep America on this hard won place. How many waters had he crossed since youth? How many friends betrayed on the way? How many trusts, dishonoured? How many loves, disappointed? And what were his thoughts when he fell, for a cheer went up in the enemy ranks when he died, though some of those close lost heart. And when he was found by his foe, next day, they were thrilled he was gone, and they threw his cold corpse in the ground, and shoveled the earth on his face that was dead to the light.

Only the day before, his former neighbour, Peter Schram, had taken aim, and brought him down with one musket ball hot to the right breast so his lungs bubbled blood and he drowned in his own red breath. Only the rain-dark day before. And it was his last afternoon, the one on which the supper hour never came for him. Around five p.m., on September 4th,

1814, he lost the last of the light. Exactly here, where I sit now, in the rushing by of cars, in this distracted hour. I conjure something of the smoke of what he was from the fumes of the here and now.

And no one, it seems, is more alone in the world, than a traitor found, but a traitor dead is less than a stone. And what his eyes could see, his tongue taste, his hands grasp, were all gone as in a poor dreamless drunkard's sleep. I hold in memory the large loop of his clear cursive, his legible letters full of hope and care, his diaries marking his days among friends. And I think, as well, of the cane he carried, lost in a closet somewhere in the world, because he gave it away while he lived. And the man who shared his initials, touched down through time until the story wore away, and the cane became forgetful as any other stick let fall by a tree struck dead. And whoever walks out the door, leans on that ghost unaware that Jonathan Woolverton of Grimsby once loved the company of Joseph Willcocks and called him friend. And if there's nothing left of the Irish boy who grieved the news of the death of his father at home across the ocean, if there's nothing remains of the brother betrayed by his blood when he found himself refused by his own, if there's nothing left of the broken-hearted suitor snubbed by the lady for his lack of station in life, if there's nothing left of the drinker's joy, and the wild and sportive youth, if there's nothing left of grief at the loss of his best friend in a duel, if there's nothing left of the past in the noise of this day, then why are we ever alive?

Cornwall August 1st, 1810.
A letter addressed to Mr. Jackson, his British Majesty's Ambassador Extraordinary to the United States, with the following verses.

Honorable Sir Francis J. Jackson

Most Honorable Sir:

I beg leave to present Your Excellency with a copy of verses on the subject of your Mission. As the Muses are not yet familiarized to the Woods of Canada the lines require much candour in the perusal.

I rejoice that I have had the honour of conversing for a few moments with Your Excellency whom I have long admired in secret. It is one of the happiest incidents of my life. Accept most Honorable Sir of my sincere prayers for the safe arrival of Your Excellency, your amiable Lady and Children in England, and a happy meeting with your numerous Friends and such a reception from Government as your transcendant abilities so richly deserve. I am Most Honorable Sir

With Profound Respect, Your Excellency's Most Obt. Humble Servant,

J. Strachan

Verses

John Strachan

1

Behold Corcyra's hateful race
Their parent Corinth spurn;
To plunge their Sires in black distress
Their rankling bosoms burn.
Like them, Columbia's Statesmen gnaw
Their British Sires with serpent jaw.
They wish to cramp the Parent State
Regardless of her glorious cause
For justice, freedom, equal laws,
As well's their own impending fate.

2

In vain these cursed children try
To prop a Despot's power.
Expos'd by Jackson's piercing eye,
Their day begins to lour.
Prescription scars her sullen coast,
And Faction shakes her blood stain'd vest
While trembling envy's cruel sting,
The produce of their poison'd hearts,
Back on themselves the sorrow darts
They sought on Englishmen to bring.

3

Lo! Britains glory future times
In rapture shall declare,
When base Columbia's dastard crimes
The wicked's meed shall share,
For grateful nations sprung from those
Who now the British views oppose,
Shall at their Fathers blush for shame,
Who sought to crush the gen'rous race
That tried to give them full redress,
And cherish'd freedom's dying flame.

4

The tribute of a rustic muse,
Exil'd from classic ground,
Let candid Jackson not refuse.
Thy name's a pleasing sound;
It tells our hearts that Britain's cause,
Intrusted to his genius bright,
More aid from truth and justice draws
Than from her sons in martial fight.

1812

SUPERIOR
CHIPPEWA HUNTING GROUND
LAKE HURON
LAKE MICHIGAN
LAKE ONTARIO
LAKE ERIE
LAKE SIMCOE
NIPISSING LAKE
WABATOUSA LAKE
Immense Forest
MIDLAND DISTRICT
Frontenac
Northumberland
Norfolk
DETROIT
POOTEWATOMES
MIAMIES
OOTAWAS
CONNECTICUT RESERVE
O H I O
Ohio River
Pittsburg
Chilicothe
Ft. Wayne
Ft. Adams
Ft. Recovery
Ft. Jefferson
Vincennes
Reference to the Townships in Canada
EASTERN DISTR
MIDLAND DISTR
HOME DISTR

Come All You Bold Canadians

Traditional

Come all you bold Canadians, I'd have you lend an ear
Concerning a fine ditty that would make your courage cheer,
Concerning an engagement—that we had at Sandwich town,
The courage of those Yankee boys so lately we pulled down.

There was a bold commander, brave General Brock by name,
Took shipping at Niagara and down to York he came,
He says, "My gallant heroes, if you'll come along with me,
We'll fight those proud Yankees in the west of Canaday!"

'Twas thus that we replied: "Along with you we'll go.
Our knapsacks we will shoulder without any more ado.
Our knapsacks we will shoulder and forward we will steer;
We'll fight those proud Yankees without either dread or fear."

We travelled all that night and a part of the next day,
With a determination to show them British play.
We travelled all that night and a part of the next day,
With a determination to conquer or to die.

Our commander sent a flag to them and unto them did say:
"Deliver up your garrison or we'll fire on you this day!"
But they would not surrender, and chose to stand their ground,
We opened up our great guns and gave them fire a round.

Their commander sent a flag to us, a quarter he did call.
"Oh, hold your guns, brave British boys, for fear you slay us all.
Our town you have at your command, our garrison likewise."
They brought their guns and ground them right down before our eyes.

And now we are all home again, each man is safe and sound.
May the memory of this conquest all through the Province sound!
Success unto our volunteers who did their rights maintain,
And to our bold commander, brave General Brock by name!

A Strike Northward: The United States Attacks British North America in the War of 1812

Raymond Souster & Les Green

The Author as Amateur Historian

In 1812, Thomas Jefferson, third president of the United States,
from 1801 to 1809, declared the following:
"The acquisition of Canada this year as far as the neighbourhood
of Quebec will be a mere matter of marching
and will give us the experience for the attack on Halifax,
the next and final expulsion of England from the American continent."

James Madison, fourth president of the United States
from 1809 to 1817, apparently held much the same views
as his predecessor. Washington Irving, the author of "Rip van Winkle",
described him at his inauguration as "a withered little applejohn".
However Madison's bosomy wife Dolly more than made up
for any of his deficiencies in wit and charm
with her warmth and high spirits which soon made her
the toast of Washington. To everyone's surprise
Madison was definitely a war hawk. He believed,
as many of his fellow countrymen did at the time,
that the American Revolution of 1783
was still incomplete as long as Britain
retained a foothold in North America.

James Madison
Fourth President of the United States

As matters now stand, our people in all three
frontier regions have very strong local interests

that can only be achieved by a war with Britain,
leading to its ultimate defeat and expulsion
from the continent. Our citizens in the South
firmly believe that fighting such a war
will eventually lead to the acquisition
of the Florida region from Britain's close ally Spain,
a territory greatly to be desired. At the same time,
on the western frontier, the war could mean
that Britain's defeat would seriously weaken
the tribes who now inhabit it and who are
very closely allied with their English friends.
This would push these troublesome savages much further west,
thus freeing up valuable land for expansion
and settlement. Finally, despite our best
trade policy efforts to prevent Britain
from acquiring much-needed products
from these United States, the situation
on the northern frontier has sadly deteriorated.
The British are still able to get these supplies
for their West Indian Colonies from either the Canadas,
or from black-guard smugglers operating freely
across the undefended border.

So it seems we must consider the possibility
of such a war for two additional important reasons.
On the one hand the British are fully occupied with Napoleon,
which must certainly take up their best soldiers.
On the other hand, we would gain a complete monopoly
over all trade with North America. This could not fail
to increase our stature in international affairs.

I do, however, face formidable obstacles which make
any undertaking that much more difficult. I'm afraid
my cabinet is divided on the question of war. Not only that,
but I'm faced with a Congress that can't make up its mind,
ignorant governors whose only purpose is to delay any decision,
and incompetent generals and ill-trained militias who flatly refuse
to fight outside of their own home states.
As if this isn't bad enough, public opinion
is apparently unprepared to support
any foreign war. Is it any wonder that
I despair of this goal ever seeing the light of day.

The Author as Amateur Historian

President Madison, nevertheless, finally won his battle with Congress,
and the politicians voted to declare war against Great Britain
on June 18, 1812. However, by a bitter stroke of irony
two days before this declaration, the British pulled in their horns
and repealed the offensive Orders in Council
pertaining to the naval blockade that had so enraged
the Americans. Sadly though, news of this development
didn't reach American shores until after the war
had well begun. As a result history was to record
the conflict that followed as Mr. Madison's war.

At the time this war began, which as it turned out
nobody really wanted, the United States of America
had a population of 8,000,000. It was by no means
a unified country as the various regions held strongly
to their own self-interests. For example, the states
of the Mississippi valley found their economies in ruins
due to the British blockade. They were no longer able

to export their prime crops of cotton and tobacco
to Europe. On the other hand, the inhabitants of Kentucky,
Ohio and the territories firmly believed that despicable British agents
were gradually goading the native tribes to resist
any further takeover of their western lands. This resulted
in much belligerent talk of teaching the savages a lesson,
a lesson they soon wouldn't forget, thereby aiding
expansion to the west and driving the British once and for all
out of North America. Uppermost in American minds
was the mistaken theory that the war now on the horizon
would somehow liberate the oppressed peoples to the north
who, they thought, deeply wanted to become Americans.

Major-General Sir Isaac Brock
British Commander

The American declaration of war on Britain
came as no surprise to me, as I was well along
in my preparations to defend the colony. The main problem
I faced was how to defend such a vast area
with what amounted to a token force consisting
of one British infantry regiment with its company of artillery,
a detachment of veterans and various untried militia units.
If it had not been for the fact that our ships
controlled the lower lakes, thus making it relatively easy
to supply the far flung outposts, this task
would have been close to impossible. Both my staff and I
had reached the conclusion that one possible American strategy
would be to cut the water link between the two Canadas
by attacking and capturing Kingston. Having achieved this,
it would seem that they would have no great difficulty
in proceeding with the capture of Montreal,

at which point we would be in a hopeless situation.
We were therefore fortunate in striking the first blow
against our enemy due to the fact that I had maintained
close communication with all my post commanders,
however distant. So it was that I dispatched the well-known trader
and voyageur William McKay by canoe to our outpost
on St. Joseph Island in northern Lake Huron.
He carroed orders that the garrison commander
should either strengthen his defences or at his discretion
launch an immediate attack on the nearby American outpost
at Fort Mackinac. Captain Charles Roberts wasted no time
going on the offensive with a mixed force of regulars,
fur traders and Indians from several tribes. The attack
was driven home on July 17, coming as a complete surprise
to our enemy who as it turned out was not even aware
that war had been declared. Their garrison surrendered
without so much as a shot being fired, raising both my spirits
and those of my men. This action had the added benefit
of now making our Indian friends, who had hitherto chosen
to remain on the sidelines, more than happy
to throw in their lot with us.

Despite this boost in morale, I was still hampered
at every turn by the actions of my superior,
Governor General George Prevost. Here was a man
who despite all logic to the contrary,
believed that the colony should remain
on a strictly defensive posture. He was convinced that
such a strategy would afford Lower Canada a better chance
of survival. In addition, there was widespread defeatism
among the politicians of whatever stripe, which at the least
was insufferable to a man in my position.

Infuriated by what I felt to be a hopeless situation,
I dispatched the following letter to the Governor's Adjutant General:

"My situation is most critical,
not from anything the enemy can do,
but from the disposition of the people—
The Population, believe me is essentially bad—
A full belief possesses them that this Province
must inevitably succumb—This Prepossession
is fatal to every exertion—Legislators, Magistrates,
Militia Officers, all, have imbibed the idea,
and are so sluggish and indifferent in all their respective offices
that the artful and active scoundrel is allowed to parade the Country
without interruption, and commit all imaginable mischief...
What a change an additional regiment would make
in this part of the Province. Most of the people have lost all confidence—
I however speak loud and stand tall, as befits a loyal soldier."

At this point in the war, I realized that it was absolutely essential
to make an alliance with the native tribes in this part
of North America. With this accomplished, I would be able
to defend this vast area with the small scattering of forces
at my disposal, and be left in a much better position
to strike successfully at the enemy. I am totally opposed
to Prevost's idea of a defensive war against the Americans
as I believe a strong show of force will encourage the native tribes
to join with us as a means of avenging the many land swindles
they have endured at the hands of the enemy. One chief in particular
seems to me to stand out among the native leaders,
and I will make every effort to convince him
to throw in his lot with his British allies.

Asylum

Keith Inman

Leon chewed slowly
his jaw jutting slightly as he mushed
the re-heated mash against the roof of his mouth.

George cracked heart-nuts
from the glass dish.

He'd told his ma
he was joining the Green Tigers.
Told her
about Asylum
for Leon.

Leon smiled,
a thin crooked wedge in a face
half opened with sunlight late for rising,
when he heard his name.
He patted George on the shoulder
as their mother hobbled with a cane
scraped the remains of her dinner
into the bucket for the pig. "I want
neither of you to go," she said,
stooped at the basin. "Is that
being selfish."

George had to grab his tea
to rinse the nut paste
        from his throat.

        Leon held his plate out for more.

When Clouds Touch Down

Keith Inman

It rained the day Seamus went in
and when he walked from under
the high-spiked Jack   flying
over the block.

His father
pulled up in a Tumbril cart,
and they rattled off. Their words
locked in their fists;
too many potholes
in the road already.

A Coach passed,
heading toward the shops.
A red haired lady glanced down
and away. Her top-hatted husband
folded his paper, stared
at Seamus, then,
the road they'd travelled.
Seamus wondered
if he'd be checking for his wallet
in a moment.

Lightning flashed over the lake.
Thunder rattled his bones.
"Look at me when I talk to you, lad.
Your Uncle's got you free. You're to join
the Rangers, now."

Along the King's Road,
clouds touched down.

War Begins

Excerpt from *The Canadian Brothers*

Major John Richardson

Several hours had passed away in the interesting discussion of their war plans, and the council was nearly concluded, when suddenly the attention both of the officers and chiefs was arrested by the report of a single cannon. From the direction of the sound, it was evident the shot had been fired from the battery placed on the southern or lakeward extremity of the Island of Bois Blanc, and as the circumstance was unusual enough to indicate the existence of some approaching cause for excitement, several of the younger of both who, from their youth, had been prevented from taking any active share in the deliberations of the day, stole, successively and unobservedly, through the large folding doors of the building, which, owing to the great heat of the weather, had been left open. After traversing about fifty yards of sward, intersecting on the high road, which, running parallel with the river, separated the council hall from the elevated bank, the officers found, collected in groups on the extreme verge of this latter and anxiously watching certain movements in the battery opposite to them, most of the troops and inferior Indians they had left loitering there at the commencement of the council. Those movements were hasty, and as of men preparing to repeat the shot, the report of which had reached them from the opposite extremity of the Island. Presently the forms, hitherto intermingled, became separate and stationary—an arm of one was next extended—then was seen to rise a flash of light, and then a volume of dense smoke, amid which the loud report found its sullen way, bellowing like thunder through some blackening cloud, while, from the peculiar nature of the sound, it was recognized, by the experienced in those matters, to have proceeded from a shotted gun.

The war in Canada had its beginning in the manner thus described, They were the first shots fired in that struggle, and although at an object little calculated to inspire much alarm, still, as the first indications of an active hostility, they were proportionably exciting to those whose lot it was thus to "break ground," for operations on a larger scale.

A Strike Northward: The United States Attacks British North America in the War of 1812

Raymond Souster & Les Green

The Author as Amateur Historian

There's no doubt that General Brock's action during the weeks
following the outbreak of war in building an alliance
with those Indian chiefs inclined to be friendly to the British cause
would play a key role in determining the outcome
of the struggle. He had to find a way to somehow increase
his meagre forces which were stretched out over three great lakes
and thousands of miles. Without the added support
of these feared native warriors, it is extremely doubtful
whether the combined British Regulars and Canadian militias
could have withstood the determined first onslaughts
of the Americans. Although he would enlist the help
of a number of native chiefs, his most successful ally
would prove to be Chief Tecumseh of the Shawnee Nation.

Tecumseh or Shooting Star
Chief of the Shawnee Nation

As early as 1809, I was actively engaged in trying to rally
my brothers against the ever-westward expansion
of American settlers, who had already tried to drive us
from our present homelands. In doing so, I faced the opposition
of many chiefs who were under the misguided impression
that they could live in peace with the Americans
and not suffer further hardship at their hands. In particular,

the Treaty of Fort Wayne by which my half-starved brothers
signed away three million acres of land for literally
no compensation deeply disturbed me. This was just more proof
that the white man could not be trusted to deal fairly with us.

Through the years of 1809 to 1811, I continued
to give warnings about the things to come
to all those who would listen. I began by telling them
how no tribe has the right to sell, even to each other,
much less to strangers. Sell the land! Why not sell the air
and the mighty sea? Didn't the Great Spirit
make them all for the use of all his children?. The only way
to stop this evil is for the red man to unite in claiming
a common and equal right in the land, as it was at first,
and should be now for it was never divided.
Before every council fire, I gave this warning:
"Brothers, if you do not unite with us, the enemy will first destroy us,
and then you will be easy prey for them. They have destroyed
many nations of red men who were not united
or friends to each other. Brothers, who are the white people
that we should fear them? They cannot run fast
and are good marks to shoot at. They are only men.
Our fathers have killed many of them. We are not women
and if forced to we will stain the earth red with their blood".

Brigadier-General William Hull
Commander of the American Army of the Northwest

After a rather strenuous stretch of duty during our War of Independence
in which I ended up as a lieutenant-colonel, I served as a judge
and state senator in Massachusetts. Then in 1805
President Jefferson appointed me as governor

of the newly created Michigan Territory, where I found
my previous military experience stood me
in good stead. On the outbreak of war in 1812,
President James Madison gave me command
of the newly-formed Army of the Northwest.

Through an unfortunate set of circumstances,
I was not made aware of the declaration of war on June 18
until July 2. Desperate to make up for lost time,
I quickly assembled my forces and launched my part of the invasion
of Upper Canada on July 12, crossing the Detroit River
without opposition and heading toward Fort Amherstburg.
At this moment misfortune reared its ugly head again
as the news finally reached me of the capture of Fort Mackinac
by the British on the 17th. Well aware that General Brock,
the enemy commander, would no doubt be heading in my direction
with considerable forces, the prudent course of action seemed to be
to fall back on the safety of Fort Detroit. Compounding our difficulties
was the added fear of an uprising by vengeful tribes in the territory
resulting in murderous attacks on the white settlers under my protection.

Major General Sir Isaac Brock
British Commander

I happened to be at the town of York on Lake Ontario
when the news of General Hull's crossing into Upper Canada
reached us. It was with a feeling of relief that I quickly assembled
a small but eager force consisting of 100 British troops of the line,
together with 300 militia volunteers. Perhaps most important of all,
200 Indian warriors lead by our new ally, Shawnee Chief Tecumseh,
were to join us later. Here Governor General Sir George Prevost
advised me not to worry about the movements in the east

by the uninspired American commander-in-chief,
Major General Henry Dearborn. Instead, I should strike out
for Fort Amherstburg to reinforce the garrison there
and disrupt the plans of the invader, General Hull.

Accordingly, once I and my little force had reached Port Dover
on Lake Erie, we set sail for Fort Amherstburg,
arriving there on August 13. Once there, we joined up
with Chief Tecumseh's band of freshly-painted warriors.
Now good luck favoured us. From captured American dispatches
we were heartened to learn that American morale at Fort Detroit
had sunk to a low level as they lived in mortal terror
of enemy Indian forces. Their supplies were also
dangerously low. Learning of this, I devised a stratagem
by which a letter would fall into Hull's hands
declaring that with 5000 Indian warriors
having already assembled at Amherstburg,
no more should be sent. Then putting my head together
with the wily Tecumseh's, to whom I now took a great liking,
we decided to strike while the iron was hot
and launch an immediate attack on Fort Detroit. I therefore dispatched
a letter demanding the surrender of the fort
in which I presented the following situation:
"The force at my disposal authorizes me to require of you
the immediate surrender of Fort Detroit. It is far from my intention
to join in a war of extermination, but you must be well aware
that the numerous body of Indian warriors who have attached themselves
to my troops will be beyond control the moment the contest commences..."

In spite of this rather outrageous letter, I was forced to concede
that my forces were markedly inferior in number
to those under Hull's command. It was here that we improvised

several far-fetched but inspired deceptions to force
the surprisingly speedy surrender of the American garrison.
These tricks included dressing up the militia
in old cast-off British uniforms and openly parading them,
lighting multiple cooking fires at night to give the impression
of a much larger army, and perhaps most successful of all,
shifting Tecumseh's warriors from place to place
accompanied by blood curdling war cries.

Meeting Between Tecumseh and Officers

Excerpt from *The Canadian Brothers*

Major John Richardson

The greeting between Tecumseh and these officers, was such as might be expected from warriors bound to each other by mutual esteem. Each held the other in the highest honor, but it was particularly remarked that while the Indian Chieftain looked up to the General with the respect he felt to be due to him, not merely as the dignified representative of his "Great Father," but as one of a heart and actions claiming his highest personal admiration, his address to his companion, whom he now beheld for the first time, was warmer, and more energetic; and as he repeatedly glanced at the armless sleeve, he uttered one of those quick ejaculatory exclamations, peculiar to his race, and indicating, in this instance, the fullest extent of approbation. The secret bond of sympathy which chained his interest to the Commodore, might have owed its being to another cause. In the countenance of the latter there was much of that eagerness of expression, and in the eye that vivacious fire, that flashed, even in repose, from his own swarthier and more speaking features; and this assimilation of character might have been the means of producing that preference for, and devotedness to, the cause of the naval commander, that subsequently developed itself in the chieftain. In a word, the General seemed to claim the admiration and the respect of the Indian—the Commodore, his admiration and friendship.

The greeting between these generous leaders was brief. When the first salutations had been interchanged, it was intimated to Tecumseh, through the medium of an interpreter, then in attendance on the General, that a war-council had been ordered, for the purpose of taking into consideration the best means of defeating the designs of the Americans, who, with a view to offensive operations, had, in the interval of the warrior's absence, pushed on a considerable force to the frontier. The council, however, had been delayed, in order that it might have the benefit of his opinions, and of his experience in the peculiar warfare which was about to be commenced.

Tecumseh acknowledged his sense of the communication with the bold frankness of the inartificial son of nature, scorning to conceal his just self-estimate beneath a veil of affected modesty. He knew his own worth, and while he over-valued not one iota of that worth, so did he not affect to disclaim a consciousness of the fact—that within his swarthy chest and active brain there beat a heart and lived a judgement, as prompt to conceive and execute as those of the proudest he that ever swayed the destinies of a warlike people. Replying to the complimentary invitation of the General, he unhesitatingly said he has done well to await his (Tecumseh's) arrival, before he determined on his course of action, and that he should now have the full benefit of his opinions and advice.

If the chief had been forcibly prepossessed in favour of the naval commander, the latter had not been less interested. Since his recent arrival, to assume the direction of the fleet, Commodore Barclay had had opportunities of seeing such of the chiefs as were then assembled at Amherstburg; but great as had been the admiration of several of these, he had been given to understand they fell far short, in every moral and physical advantage, of what their renowned leader would be found to posses, when, on his return from the expedition in which he was engaged, fitting opportunity should be had of bringing them in personal proximity. This admission was now made in the fullest sense, and as the warrior moved away to give the greeting to the several chiefs, and conduct them to the council hall, the gallant sailor could not refrain from expressing, in the warmest terms to General Brock, as they moved slowly forward with the same intention, the enthusiastic admiration excited in him by the person, the manner, and the bearing, of the noble Tecumseh.

Again the cannon from the battery and the shipping pealed forth their thunder. It was the signal for commencement of the council, and the scene at that moment was one of the most picturesque that can well be imagined. The sky was cloudless, and the river, no longer ruffled by the now motionless barks of the recently arrived Indians, yet obeying the action of the tide, offered, as it glided onward to the lake, the image of a flood of quick-silver; while, in the distance, that lake itself, smooth as a mirror, spread far and wide. Close under the bank yet lingered the canoes, emptied only of their helmsmen (the chiefs of the several tribes,) while, with strange tongues and wilder gestures, the warriors of these, as they rested on their paddles, greeted the loud report of the cannon—now watching with eager eye the flashes from the vessel's sides, and now upturning their gaze, and following with wild surprise, the deepening volumes of smoke that passed immediately over their heads, from the guns of the battery, hidden from their view by the elevated and overhanging bank. Blended with each discharge arose the wild yell, which they, in such a movement of novel excitement, felt it impossible to control, and this, answered from the Indians above and born in echo almost to the American shore, had in it something indescribably startling. On the bank itself the effect was singularly picturesque. Here were to be seen the bright uniforms of the British officers, at the head of whom was the tall and martial figure of General Brock, furthermore conspicuous from the full and drooping feather that fell gracefully over his military hat, mingled with the wilder and more fanciful head dresses of the chiefs. Behind these again, and sauntering at a pace that showed them to have no share in the deliberative assembly, whither those we have just named were now proceeding amid the roar of artillery, yet mixed together in nearly as great dissimilarity of garb, were to be seen numbers of the inferior warriors and of the soldiery, while, in various directions, the games recently abandoned by the adult Indians, were now resumed by mere boys. The whole picture was one of strong animation, contrasting as it did with the quiet of the little post on the Island, where some twelve or fifteen men, composing the strength of the detachment, were now sitting or standing on the battery, crowned, as well as the fort and shipping, and in compliment to the newly arrived Indians, with the colours of England.

Scene Fifth—Sandwich, on the Detroit—A Room in the Baby Mansion

excerpt from *Tecumseh, a Drama*

Charles Mair

Enter GENERAL BROCK, COLONELS PROCTOR, GLEGG, BABY, MACDONEL, NICHOL, ELLIOT and other Officers

BABY:
Welcome! thrice welcome!
Brave Brock, to Sandwich and this loyal roof!
Thank God, your oars, those weary levers bent
In many a wave, have been unshipped at last;
And, now, methinks those lads who stemmed the flood
Would boldly face the fire.

BROCK:
I never led
Men of more cheerful and courageous heart,
But for whose pluck foul weather and short seas,
'Twere truth to say, had made an end of us.
Another trial will, I think, approve
The manly strain this Canada hath bred.

PROCTOR: '
Tis pity that must be denied them now,
Since all our enemies have left our shores.

BROCK:
No, by my soul, it shall not be denied!
Our foe's withdrawal hath a magnet's power

And pulls my spirit clean into his fort.
But I have asked you to confer on this.
What keeps Tecumseh?

ELLIOTT:
'Tis his friend, Lefroy,
Who now rejoins him, after bootless quest
Of Iena, Tecumseh's niece.

BROCK:
Lefroy!
I had a gentle playmate of that name
In Guernsey, long ago.

BABY:
It may be he.
I know him, and, discoursing our affairs,
Have heard him speak of you, but in a strain
Peculiar to the past.

BROCK:
He had in youth
All goods belonging to the human heart,
But fell away to Revolution's side—
Impulsive ever, and o'er prompt to see
In kings but tyrants, and in laws but chains.
I have not seen or heard of him for years.

BABY:
The very man!

BROCK: ‘
Tis strange to find him here!

ELLIOTT:
He calls the red men freedom's last survival;
Says truth is only found in Nature's growth—
His first intention, ere false knowledge rose
To frame distinctions, and exhaust the world.

BROCK:
Few find like him the substance of their dreams.
But, Elliot, let us seek Tecumseh now.
Stay, friends, till we return.

[Exeunt BROCK and ELLIOTT]

GLEGG:
How odd to find
An old friend in this fashion!

PROCTOR:
Humph! a fool
Who dotes on forest tramps and savages.
Why, at the best, they are the worst of men;
And this Tecumseh has so strained my temper,
So over-stept my wishes, thrid my orders,
That I would sooner ask the devil's aid
Than such as his.

NICHOL:
Why, Brock is charmed with him!
And, as you saw, at Amherstburg he put
Most stress upon opinion when he spoke.

MACDONELL:
Already they've determined on assault.

PROCTOR:
Then most unwisely so! There are no bounds
To this chief's rashness, and our General seems
Swayed by it too, or rashness hath a twin.

NICHOL:
Well, rashness is the wind of enterprise.
And blows its banners out. But here they come
Who dig beneath their rashness for their reasons.

Re-enter GENERAL BROCK and COLONEL ELLIOTT accompanied by TECUMSEH, conversing

TECUMSEH:
We have been much abused! and have abused.
Our fell destroyers too—making our wrongs
The gauge of our revenge. And, still forced back
From the first justice and native right,
Ever revenge hath sway. This we would void,
And, by common boundary, prevent.
So, granting that a portion of our own
Is still our own, then let that portion be
Confirmed by sacred treaty to our tribes.
This is my sum of asking—you have ears!

BROCK:
Nay, then, Tecumseh, speak of it no more!
My promise is a pledge, and from a man
Who never turned his back on friend or foe.
The timely service you have done our cause,
Rating not what's to come, would warrant it.
So, if I live, possess your soul of this—
No treaty for a peace, if we prevail,

Will bear a seal that doth not guard your rights.
Here, take my sash, and wear it for my sake—
Tecumseh can esteem a soldier's gift.

TECUMSEH:
Thanks, thanks, my brother, I have faith in you;
My life is at your service!

BROCK:
Gentlemen,
Have you considered my proposal well
Touching the capture of Detroit by storm?
What say you, Colonel Procter?

PROCTOR:
I object!
'Tis true, the enemy has left our shores,
But what a sorry argument is this!
For his withdrawal, which some sanguine men,
Jumping all other motives, charge to fear,
Prudence, more deeply searching, lays to craft.
Why should a foe, who far outnumbers us,
Retreat o'er this great river, save to lure
Our poor force after him? And, having crossed—
Our weakness seen, and all retreat cut off—
What would ensure but absolute surrender,
Or sheer destruction? 'Tis too hazardous!
Discretion balks at such a mad design.

BROCK:
What say the rest?

1st OFFICER:
I fear 'tis indiscreet.

2nd OFFICER:
'Twould be imprudent with our scanty force.

BROCK:
What say you, Nichol, to my foolish scheme?

NICHOL:
I think it is feasible and prudent too.
Hull's letters, captured by Tecumseh, prove
His soldiers mutinous, himself despondent
And dearly Rumour loves the wilderness,
Which gives a thousand echoes to a tongue
That ever swells and magnifies our strength.
And in this flux, we take him, on the hinge
Of two uncertainties—his force and ours.
So, weighed, objections fall; and our attempt,
Losing its grain of rashness, takes its rise
In clearest judgement, whose effect will nerve
All Canada to perish, ere she yield.

BROCK:
My very thoughts! What says Tecumseh now?

TECUMSEH:
I say attack the fort! This very night
I'll cross my braves, if you decide on this.

BROCK:
Then say no more! Glegg, take a flag of truce,

And bear to Hull this summons to surrender.
Tell him Tecumseh and his force are here—
A host of warriors brooding on their wrongs,
Who, should resistance flush them to revenge,
Would burst from my control like wind-borne fire,
And match on earth the miseries of hell.
But, should he yield, his safety is assured.
Tell him Tecumseh's word is pledged to this,
Who, though his temperate will in peace is law,
Yet casts a loose rein to enforcèd rage.
Add what your fancy dictates; but the stress
Place most on what I speak of—this he fears,
And these same fears, well wrought upon by you,
May prove good workers for us yet.

GLEGG:
I go,
And shall acquit myself as best I can.

[Exit GLEGG]

BROCK:
Tecumseh, wonder not at such a message!
The guilty conscience of your foes is judge
Of their deserts, and hence 'twill be believed.
The answer may be "nay," so to our work—
Which perfected, we shall confer again,
Then cross at break of morn.

[Exeunt all but TECUMSEH]

TECUMSEH:
This is a man!

And our Great Father, waking from his sleep,
Has sent him to our aid. Master of Life,
Endue my warriors and with double strength!
May the wedged helve be faithful to the axe,
The arrow fail not, and the flint be firm!
That our great vengeance, like the whirlwind fell,
May cleave through thickets of our enemies
A broad path to our ravaged lands again.

[Exit]

Description of Troops Moving by Water

excerpt from *The Canadian Brothers*

Major John Richardson

Seldom has there been witnessed a more romantic or picturesque sight than that presented by an expedition of bateaux moving across one of the Canadian lakes, during a season of profound calm. The uniform and steady pull of the crew, directed in their time by the wild chaunt of the steersman, with whom they ever and anon join in full chorus—the measured plash of the oars into the calm surface of the water—the joyous laugh and rude, but witty, jest of the more youthful and buoyant of the soldiery, from whom, at such moments, although in presence of their officers, the trammels of restraint are partially removed—all these, added to the inspiriting sight of their gay scarlet uniforms, and the dancing of the sunbeams upon their polished arms, have a tendency to call up impressions of a wild interest, tempered only by the recollection that many of those who move gaily on, as if to a festival—bright in hope as though the season of existence were to last for ever, may never more set eye upon the scenes they are fast quitting, with the joyousness produced by the natural thirst of the human heart for adventure, and a love of change.

Sea Letters Home

Denis Robillard

Note: This is an imaginary letter sent by an officer aboard ship to his wife back in England in the early stages of the War of 1812.

Dearest Anne:

It has been difficult to make the sea my friend.
I have endured so much So much in the abyss
Of darkness and misery.
Even the lowly rat refuses to acknowledge my presence
In these dank dark confines.
The sleep quarters are unbearable, the food even more so.
These men accustomed to sacrifice grow surly and unkempt.
Of late we have been forced to eat horsemeat brought aboard
from the coast of Halifax. The meat is soaked in saline au jus.
It will have to do.
The bread crawls with weevils and bugs.

Sometimes at night I swear I see human forms
Walking upon the mist-obliterated floorboards of this forsaken ship.
In my eye's fancy I carve things into conjured shapes.
O the shape of you Sweet Remembrancer.
You my raven haired maiden who has suffered so much in this war,
For this war, and waiting still for your salty legged lover.

The nights are intolerable. Bed ridden and alone I suffer.
Bed ridden and alone you suffer.
On these inky seas
where only the stars have called me friend, I dream this night
Of hands upon your body to help me choke out these sea sighs
And the juggernaut calamities of liquid voyage.

Yours as ever, a sea soldier lost

Battle of Detroit

excerpt from *The Canadian Brothers*

Major John Richardson

It is impossible to review the whole tenor of General Brock's conduct, on the occasion more immediately before our notice, and fail to be struck by the energy and decision of character which must have prompted so bold an enterprise. To understand fully the importance of the operation it will be necessary to take a partial survey of the position of affairs anterior to this period. When the announcement of the American declaration of war first reached the Michigan frontier, the garrisons of Amherstburg and Detroit were nearly equal in strength, neither of them exceeding five hundred men; but the scale was soon made preponderate immeasurably in favor of the latter, by the sudden arrival of a force of upwards two thousand men. General Hull, who was in command of that army immediately crossed over into Canada, occupying the village of Sandwich as his headquarters, and pouring his wild Kentuckians over the face of the country which they speedily laid under contribution. Instead, however, of marching without delay upon Amherstburg, as ill defended as it was weakly garrisoned, he contented himself with pushing forward skirmishers, who amused themselves during the day, against an advanced post of regulars, militia and Indians, stationed for the defence of an important pass, and retired invariably on the approach of night. This pass, the Canard bridge—and the key to Amherstburg—was, at this period, the theatre of several hot and exciting affairs. In this manner passed the whole of the month of July.

Meanwhile, intelligence having been conveyed to General Brock, then in command of the centre division of the army, of the danger with which Amherstburg was threatened. He immediately embarked what remained of the Regiment occupying that post, with from one hundred and fifty to two hundred choice Militia, in boats he had caused to be collected for the purpose, and, coasting along the lake, made such despatch that he arrived at Amherstburg only a few days after General Hull, in his turn apprized of the advance of this reinforcement, had recrossed the river, and with the majority of his force, taken refuge within the fortifications of Detroit. Thus was that portion of Upper Canada, which by Proclamation of the American General, had already been incorporated with, and become a portion of the United States, resorted to its original possessors.

Not a moment did the English Commander lose, in following up the advantage resulting from this mark of timidity in his opponent. As soon as he had arrived and ascertained the true state of affairs, he issued orders for the march of the whole force to Sandwich, and, having explained in council with the Indian Chiefs, the main features of his plan of attack, proceeded to carry it into instant execution. His arrival at Amherstburg was about the 13th of August, so that until the morning of his meditated attack scarcely three days were occupied in preparations, including the march to Sandwich, a distance of eighteen miles.

It is difficult to imagine that the English General could, in any way have anticipated so easy a conquest. He had no reason to undervalue the resolution of the enemy, and yet he appears to have been fully sanguine of the success of his undertaking. Possibly he counted much on his own decision and judgement, which, added to the confidence reposed in him by all ranks and branches of the expedition, he might have felt fully adequate to the overthrow of the mere difficulty arising from superiority of numbers. Whatever his motive, or however founded his expectations of success, the service he performed was eminent, since he not merely relieved Amherstburgh, the key of Upper Canada, from all immediate danger, but at a single blow annihilated the American power throughout the extensive frontier. That this bold measure, powerfully contrasted as it was with his own previous vacillation of purpose, had greatly tended to intimidate the American General, and to render him distrustful of his own resources, there can be little doubt. The destructive fire from the well served breaching batteries, was moreover instanced as an influencing cause of the capitulation.

In justice to many American officers of rank, and to the Garrison generally, it must be admitted that the decision of their leader, if credence might be given to their looks and language, was any thing but satisfactory to them, and it must be confessed that it must have been mortifying in the extreme to have yielded without a blow a fortress so well provided with the means of defence. What the result would have been, had the British columns mounted to the assault, it is impossible to say. That they would have done their duty is beyond all question, but there is no reason to believe the Americans, under a suitable commander, would have failed in theirs. Superiority of numbers and position was on the one side: a daring Chief, an ardent desire of distinction, and the impossibility of retreat without humiliation, on the other.

In alluding thus to the capitulation of Detroit, we beg not to be understood as either reflecting on the American character, or unduly exalting our own. Question of personal bravery there was none, since no appeal was made to arms; but the absence of sanguinary event left in high relief the daring of the British Commander, whose promptitude and genius alone secured to him so important yet bloodless a conquest.

River Scout

Keith Inman

It was warm for Spring. The rivers
raced with run-off. And, the horses
were nervous. William led them
down a winding curve of the escarpment's
limestone gravity of hammered stratii.

He was to meet Brock for supper,
and the eventual argument on continental
shift, and whose fault that was.
                    All William knew
was that the earth had endured more
catastrophe than all the cracked tea cups
in China, and India for that matter.

They rode on along one of the many
small cataracts that channeled
the peninsula into miled sections.
A dense fog ceilinged the lower
fields of stubbled-grass and orchards.

Beyond hedgerows and side lanes,
oil lamps from sheds and houses
shone upward in narrow shafts, holding
the evenings canvas in place,
as a sword of the moon sheened fearward
from the fortress pines to the Southeast.

They rode quickly, picking up speed,
until the horses suddenly reared

at an oxbow corner to the river. Toads
covered the path; were being squashed
under the horses hooves. Didn't
they know about crossed lines?

The men dismounted onto the slippery mass;
they sniffed for ambush.   Silence
drifted from the embanked marsh.
The horses stamped. On this cricket-less night,
wet hides thumped their pillared legs.

A Strike Northward: The United States Attacks British North America in the War of 1812

Raymond Souster & Les Green

The Author as Amateur Historian

Faced with all these seemingly growing threats
and a final all-out cannonade, General Hull, to everyone's surprise
meekly surrendered on August 16, 1812, thus making it
the second bloodless victory in the war. For General Brock
this meant the capture of many American prisoners,
but of even more importance, much needed supplies. As well,
it brought even more native tribes over to the British side,
a result of immeasurable importance to the future
of the two Canadas. For his part in the victory,
General Brock was awarded a knighthood, but sadly
the news of it would not reach him before his untimely death.

Major General Sir Isaac Brock
British Commander

Fresh from our victory at Fort Detroit, I hurried back
to the Niagara frontier, eager to continue the momentum
of battle. Intelligence told me that Sacket's Harbour
at the extreme eastern end of Lake Ontario was the site
of a vigorous program of American ship-building,
as our enemy still hoped to control the lower lakes.
But due to the meddling interference of our Governor General,
Sir George Prevost, my plans were thwarted
for the time being. This nincompoop had the audacity to sign

a short armistice with the now American commander,
Major General Henry Dearborn, thus giving our foes precious time
to regroup and plan further excursions against us.
Faced with this frustration, I could do little more
than attempt to strengthen our key points along the Niagara River
which included Fort Erie and Fort George.

Thus it was that on the morning of October 13
I was awakened by the noise of distant cannon fire,
which signaled to me that our enemy was again
on the move. I quickly mounted my horse Albert
and galloped toward what I now knew would be a battle
in progress. On my arrival I found that American militiamen
had already crossed the Niagara River at Queenston
and encountering little organized resistance
had succeeded in taking up positions on the heights above.
Hastily organizing my small force of regulars and militia
and putting myself at their head, I waved my sword
and we stormed up the hill in splendid fashion.

Major General Stephen Van Rensselaer III
United States Army

Although I was a Federalist and strongly opposed to the war
against the British which erupted in June, at that time I was hoping
to run for the governorship of New York under a Federalist platform.
However, my sly opponent, the then-governor Daniel D. Tompkins,
apparently fearful of my chances in the upcoming election,
now seized upon the fact that I was already a general
in the militia. By arranging to have command of the U.S. Army of the Centre
offered to me, he gave me little choice as a loyal American
but to accept this new challenge. These forces consisted largely
of militiamen like myself, who had no previous experience

in war. My second-in-command Brigadier-General Alexander Smyth,
well aware of this fact and repeatedly ignored my instructions,
hoping thereby to somehow cause me to lose my command.

With all this in mind and with the knowledge that the British
were rapidly fortifying Queenston Heights directly across the river,
I made what was perhaps a hasty and ill-advised decision to attack
from our Lewiston side, an action my officers
were heartily in favour of. Much to my surprise,
the attack exceeded all my expectations and we swept aside
the British defenders, speedily occupying the whole crest
of the heights. We didn't have to wait very long
for the British counterattack led by their commander
General Brock. This was a valiant but perhaps foolish attempt
with a very small force, which we quickly drove back
to the village of Queenston below. It was during this skirmish
that I was badly wounded, and in some puzzling manner command
was assumed by Lieutenant-Colonel Winfield Scott. I would later learn
that Brock had been killed in the attempt. With the arrival shortly after
of some British regulars and militiamen at the village of Queenston,
the British launched a second attack, which we easily beat back.

The Author as Amateur Historian

Still licking their wounds from two unsuccessful attacks
and the death of General Isaac Brock in the initial charge
and acting on the advice of their newly arrived Six Nations allies,
the now British commander Major-General Roger Sheaffe,
tried a new strategy. Moving west under cover, his mixed force
finally found a path leading up the escarpment
to the level ground above on the enemy's flank. Totally unprepared
to meet a threat from this quarter, the Americans
were completely surprised. A general panic set in

and after a single British volley and charge
the Americans now trapped under Winfield Scott
had no choice but to surrender. Their former commander
Van Rensselaer, although badly wounded, somehow
managed to escape. Shortly thereafter he resigned his commission.

The death of General Isaac Brock came as a shock
to the people of Upper Canada and no doubt strengthened
their resolve to defend their native soil. It also has to be reported
that the death of Brock's ally Chief Tecumseh at Detroit,
went almost unnoticed earlier that same October.
Tjos was under rather sad circumstances
at the Battle of the Thames near Moraviantown.
The war, for all intents and purposes, was over
for that year, with both sides planning future strategies.

Death of Brock

excerpt from *The Canadian Brothers*

Major John Richardson

In October of the same year, a numerous body of Americans, principally troops of the line, had been collected under the orders of General Van Ransaellar, and advantage was taken of a dark night in October to push them across the river, with a view to the occupation of the commanding heights above the village of Queenston. In this, favored by circumstances, the enemy were eminently successful.—They carried the batteries, and at day break the heights were to be seen covered with their battalions, before whom were thrown out a considerable body of tirailleurs, or riflemen. At the first alarm, the little detachment stationed at Queenston, marched out to dislodge them; but such was the impatient gallantry of General Brock, who had succeeded to the command of this line of frontier, that without waiting for the main body from Fort George to come up, he threw himself at the head of the flank companies of the Forty-Ninth, and moving forward in double quick time, soon came within sight of the enemy.

Among the General's Aides-de-Camps, was Henry Grantham, who having succeeded in making his escape at the fatal defeat of the Moravian Village, with a few men of his company, had in the absence of his Regiment, (then prisoners of war) and from considerations of personal esteem, been attached as a supernumerary to his staff. With him at this moment was the light hearted De Courcy, and as the young men rode a little in rear of their Chief, they were so rapt in admiration of his fine form and noble daring, (as he still kept dashing onward, far in advance even of the handful of troops who followed eagerly and rapidly in his rear,) that they utterly forgot the danger to which he was exposed.

On arriving at the ascent, the General for a moment reined in his charger, in order to give time to the rear to close in, then removing and waving his plumed hat,

"Hurrah, Forty-Ninth!" he exclaimed, in language suited to those he addressed. "Up these heights lies our road—on ourselves depends the victory. Not a shot till we gain the summit—then three cheers for old England—a volley—and the bayonet must do the rest!"

So saying, he resumed his hat, and wheeling his horse, once more led his gallant little band up the hill.

But it was not likely that the Americans would suffer the approach of so determined an enemy without attempting to check their progress in the most efficient manner. Distinguished from those around him by his commanding air, not less than by the military insignia that adorned him, the person of the General was at once recognized for one bearing high rank, and as such became an object of especial attention to the dispersed riflemen. Shot after shot flew past the undaunted officer, carrying death into the close ranks that followed noiselessly in his rear, yet without harming him. At length he was seen by his Aides-de-Camps, both of whom had kept their eyes upon him, to reel in his saddle. An instant brought the young men to his side, De Courcy on his right and Grantham on his left hand. They looked up into his face. It was suffused with the hues of death. A moment afterwards and he fell from his horse, with his head reclining upon the chest of Harry Grantham. There was a momentary halt in the advancing column; all were dismayed at the dreadful event.

De Courcy and Grantham. having abandoned their horses, now bore their beloved leader to the side of the road, in order to admit of the unimpeded progress of the men. Even in his last moments the General had no other thought but for the duty in which he was engaged.

"Bid them move on, De Courcy," he said in a faint voice, as he remarked the sudden check which had been given to the advance by his fall. Then, as if obedient to the command, they renewed the ascent, each man eyeing him as he passed with a look in which deep sorrow and a desire to avenge his death were intimately blended. "Forty-Ninth, I have served with you from boyhood, and if ye would I die with honor this day—carry those heights."

There was a deep murmur through the ranks of both companies, that showed how each and all were affected by this appealing address of the dying officer. At that moment there arose a loud shout from the hill, as of triumph at the fall of him they mourned. They answered it with the fierce expression of men resolved to turn that shout of triumph into a cry of woe; and excited, maddened, infuriated, yet with the steadiness of movement that claimed the admiration even of their enemies, dashed, heedless of the galling fire of the riflemen, up the steep.

Left alone with the dying General, it became a first consideration with the young officers to convey him (provided he could bear removal) to some spot out of reach of the enemy's fire, where he might breathe his last moments in peace.

Yankees

S. A. McCormick

Brutal wind and snow
were not torment enough
in York two winters past
When ice did thaw at last
we used our hands to sow,
our implements held hostage
in King's stores, thanks
to General Simcoe and
senseless British hoarding

So was it great surprise in summer
Yankees declared war on England
when we should scythe first cut hay?
An omen bell, instead we fight
a British war in Upper Canada
alongside native men, sure valued
for their warring acumen

October 1812 knelled
the death of General Brock
in blackness still we survived
another winter without shovels
in ragged blankets, we lost
no children, were blessed
In spring the Yankees came
Small blessing that our poverty
led them past our door
to richer bounty

Our town neighbours suffered more
Yankees stripped them bare, stole
their stores, houses sacked, and
General Simcoe's hoards slung
over backs, carted to the shore
tools we could have used
forks to stab Yankee eyes
loaded to their greedy ships
More than we should bear

Some say they overloaded cargo
pigs and flour tossed overboard

The Battle of Queenston Heights
Traditional

Upon the Heights of Queenston one dark October day,
Invading foes were marshalled in battle's dread array.
Brave Brock looked up the rugged steep and planned a bold attack;
"No foreign flag shall float," said he, "above the Union Jack."

His loyal-hearted soldiers were ready every one,
Their foes were thrice their number, but duty must be done.
They started up the fire-swept hill with loud resounding cheers,
While Brock's inspiring voice rang out: "Push on, York Volunteers!"

But soon a fatal bullet pierced through his manly breast,
And loving friends to help him around the hero pressed;
"Push on," he said, "Do not mind me!"—and ere the set of the sun
Canadians held the rugged steep, the victory was won.

Each true Canadian soldier laments the death of Brock;
His country told its sorrow in monumental rock;
And if a foe should e'er invade our land in future years,
His dying words will guide us still: "Push on, brave Volunteers!"

The Ballad of Queenston Heights

Francis Sparshott

The Yankees stood on Queenston Heights
in coats of modest grey
and Brock has brought his fencibles
to make them go away

Who is that sweating officer
waving a useless sword?
That's General Sir Isaac Brock
who wants to be a Lord

God bless the British soldier
who wears a coat of red
it makes a splendid target
and so they shot him dead

They laughed to see the fencibles
run down the hill in fear
but Roger Sheaffe has scaled the Heights
and caught them in the rear

Who is this cool young officer
who shoots us through the heart?
That's Major General Roger Sheaffe
who wants to be a Bart

Now all you bold Canadian girls
remember Queenston Heights
it's thanks to such as Brock and Scheaffe
that you sleep safe at nights

Cool Sheaffe was made a Baronet
and back to England sent
but Brock still stands on Queenston Heights
upon his monument

Brock

Charles Sangster
October 13, 1859

One voice, one people, one in heart
 And soul, and feeling, and desire!
 Re-light the smouldering martial fire,
 Sound the mute trumpet, strike the lyre,
 The hero deed can not expire,
  The dead still play their part.

Raise high the monumental stone!
 A nation's fealty is theirs,
 And we are the rejoicing heirs,
 The honoured sons of sires whose cares
 We take upon us unawares,
  As freely as our own.

We boast not of the victory,
 But render homage, deep and just,
 To his—to their—immortal dust,
 Who proved so worthy of their trust
 No lofty pile nor sculptured bust
  Can herald their degree.

No tongue need blazon forth their fame—
 The cheers that stir the sacred hill
 Are but mere promptings of the will
 That conquered then, that conquers still;
 And generations yet shall thrill
  At Brock's remembered name.

Some souls are the Hesperides
    Heaven send to guard the golden age,
    Illuming the historic page
    With records of their pilgrimage;
    True Martyr, Hero, Poet, Sage:
        And he was one of these.

Each in his lofty sphere sublime
    Sits crowned above the common throng.
    Wrestling with some Pythonic wrong,
    In prayer, in thunder, thought, or song;
    Briaereus-limbed, they sweep along,
        The Typhons of the time.

Gentleman Volunteer

Joseph Willocks at the Battle of Queenston Heights

John B. Lee

Sheaffe woke us and we rode
or walked
against the flow
a human river out of step with natural time
or widdershins with water winding back the hour
and the sun
we were approaching our own death
as man by man we thought
as if the cattle dust
beneath our morning ramp
were but a trampling up of souls.
How man in the gorge were we...
and I upon my mount
imaginary statue on a plinth of land
the limestone generations
heavy in the press of ages
and if we feared to die
above the river roar
if we feared primordial things
in that the last
and less than gentle night
we heard
the crack of distant guns
like sticks that snap in storm
we heard the cloud-burst cannon
and felt the shock and after-shock
that shakes the breathing ribs both ways

and makes the heart an apple in a wind-wrecked tree.
We but arrived
and all the chaos
of a general death
shivered up the heights
as if in the gathering back
of a caught and broken chain a link were snagged
upon a root
and then we stood our ground
and then we made
each musket volley count
and took revenge
and saw the enemy spill
their courage
like a stone that wrecks its path
upon a hill
and dozens drowned for home
as sheep ticks will
that cannot hold their life
and float a fatal memory
of what they were
mere soldiers
of a lost belief
they tumbled back
and then the day was ours.

And if by one regret I'm known
I'm known by this
that I was blind to how the war of little men
is not the same for large.
How like a toy I was
who felt the hand of God

reach down
to set aright a few
and I'm but made of tin
and painted
like a rust-wet nail
and sent away
to click a cricket song
while others
hold the proud attention
of the wheel of the world
and remain champions
to their shadows in the sun and stone.

excerpted from *In the Terrible Weather of Guns*

1813

SUPERIOR
CHIPPEWAY
CHIPPEWA HUNTING GROUND
UPPER
LOWER
WILDERNESS
WARATOUBA LAKE
TEMISCAMING
N.W.C. House
NIPISSING LAKE
Immense Forest
CANADA
EASTERN
NEMONIS
LAKE HURON
LAKE SIMCOE
MIDLAND DISTRICT
HOME DISTRICT
Northumberland
Frontenac
Durham
York
LAKE ONTARIO
Oswego
LAKE MICHIGAN
MICHIGAN
OTTAWAS
CHIPPEWAS
DETROIT
Brownstown
LAKE ERIE
POOTEWATOMES
MIAMIES
Ft. Wayne
CONNECTICUT RESERVE
OHIO
Pittsburg
Ohio River
Vincennes
Reference to the Townships in Canada
EASTERN DISTR
MIDLAND DISTR
HOME DISTR

How the World Began

Don Gutteridge

The ravages of General Harrison in Ohio and Indiana, like those of 'Mad Anthony' Wayne twenty years before, are visible all that dreary autumn. Cal hears the old tales and the fresh ones. As the cold sets in early, blowing the woods leafless and desolate they cannot help but bear witness to the Indians arriving daily from the slaughter-pens of the Ohio. They come ashore along the Detroit on rafts or logs or stray planks, whole families of them: burned out, their corn razed or plundered, husbands and fathers killed in fierce bush-combat: youngsters and squaws and a few frail elders. All are famished, dazed: they drift past the camps too weak or hopeless to plead or be afraid of blue uniforms or stoke the rage they would need to reclaim their ravaged humanness. Those who have already arrived and fed and revived enough to feel their individual agonies, would wander out on the trails to meet the newcomers, peering into faces, afraid to speak, but gently guiding them to the meadowlands Brock has reserved for them before his departure. Cal visits them, once. He feels ashamed to give them food, their bodies accept it so greedily, but what is to be gained? Their misery is absolute: flesh bruised, scabbed, festering; bones splintered by lead shot; faces pocked and swollen, teeth broken; children with bellies big as cows' bladders, dead-eyed, whimperless; the tribes and their proud tongues all mixed—blasphemously entangled, a sorrowful cacophony. And the maids—damson-eyed, tawny, Trill's age—are fed extra, fed the best meat, kept plump for the flesh-dens of the friends troops in blue jackets.

The warriors—those few who have fled and counter-fought and retreated north and had no time to mourn their dead or broken clans or scorched fields—gather in clumps on Bois Blanc island and whet the edge of their monumental anger.

Above the moving column the sun shines intrepidly but is powerless in the January cold. The road winds through light woods but the frozen Lake is easily seen through it. It must go half as far as the world itself, Cal surmises. The ice upon it is buckled and bone-fractured. In the night it will groan like a beaten ox. Miles eastward where the ice ends must be the water itself, steel-blue and bottomless, stretching to the very point where the sun has risen only hours before.

Here and there they see strips of cleared land, cottages, meadows under shawls of snow. The drifting on the road keeps the column moving erratically. Cal chafes whenever they halt. Often for an hour or more. Men curse, their curses reverberate; no one knows what has broken down, got stuck, decided to die in its tracks. Their unit assists a drover in hauling his supply-sled out of a crevasse. The mule is already dead, frozen stiff in the black water, its tongue stuck out. Lapin chuckles: "Life of a soldier, eh?"

By the late afternoon they are close enough behind the regulars to spot the village up ahead. The Pottawatomie are already there, coming down on it from the bush above, wordless and solemn. The regulars, scarlet and brass and glittering flintlocks, maintain their disciplined pace. They have no curiosity. Are they, too, afraid? Have they any other hope than this?

The settlement is called Brownstown. Not a soul emerges from the log-houses, sill-deep in drifted snow. No woodsmoke stains the pure transparency of the sky. Where are the good citizens? The shouts of praise and deliverance?

"They've all skedaddled in the other direction." Lapin tells him. "To the Yankees." He laughs wryly: "Who don't speak a lick of French."

The word 'traitor' is passed up and down the line above the neighing and the clatter and the grumbling. It doesn't matter; the enemy up ahead is real, etched in malice, bent on its own liberating bravery.

Lapin smiles at his men, older than his years. "It's the farms they care about," he says, "not us or the Yankees. They're like these Indians here." He waves towards the Pottawatomie and Wyandot clustering along the wooded fringes of the village, making their separate camp, keeping their hatred distinct and incorruptible. Cal admires them: they inhabit a world of cruel and exhilarating absolutes. Lapin gives a wry grin, feeling his age, the distance he has travelled already. "They're just like Roundhead or Tecumseh; they gotta choose the winner, or else."

The all-night bivouac is hard on the troops. The rapture of marching forth, flags flying, redcoats splendid in the vanguard, the surge of expectation, blood pounding and eager for the contest—all this is soon dissipated. Cold grub, thin tea, porous tents in a blizzard that heaves and buckles. Some tents are blown apart. Cal spends the hours before dawn crouched next to Lapin in a grove of some sort under a buffalo robe. Here there is no whisper of sleigh-runners over the virgin snow of Bear Creek nor Trill's song of intense delight nor Maman's sighs of contentment under a New Year's moon. Nearby a boy-man sobs in his sleep. Through the ragged squalls they glimpse the amber squares of cottage-windows, hear the officers in full, confident chorus. Cal has a dream.

The sun arrives to welcome blue sky. Campfires blazen forth. A cache of beef-cattle is discovered in the woodlot, slaughtered, and served up—scorched and dripping—for breakfast. Lapin plays a rousing ditty on his harmonica. Men shout, laugh. exchange insults, prime their courage. Lumbering, zigzag, impatient—Proctor's army, a thousand-strong, and all its baggage and accoutrements swing into line and march ahead south-east to the River Raisin, where history awaits them. Cal hears the regulars up ahead break into a marching-song. The bugles and drums join in. The forest has not heard such thrilling pronouncement, its echoes sail down the endless lake, the news of this coming is trumpet-loud against the farthest horizon. The men tramp smartly to the beat of the drum, stronger and braver than the beat of their individual hearts. All day they march in this manner. When the drums rest, the beat is maintained. The soldiers hum. Lapin's men will be second to none. When they halt briefly, no one speaks. It would be taken as sacrilege.

They are to attack at first light. But again Cal's world has crumbled. Lapin's unit is ordered to cover the rear of the attacking force, to guard the only road against possible flanking manoeuvres ("Through that bush?" Lapin laughs), and to protect the refugees, those farmers and townsmen whose homes are about to be destroyed in the blazing exchange of battle. (It was late in the day when Lapin relayed the command to halt. "We're supposed to make light camp right here. Frenchtown's somewhere down-river. We go at dawn!") But of course as it turns out, this unit is not destined to be covered in any glory.

In the last hour of light Cal begs information from every soldier or drover or gunner who passes the picket they have set up in among some small trees, where they will be able to watch the road both ways and not be seen. Everyone else is on the move, bound for combat. Shouts have become hoarse whispers: distempered, curt, anxious.

"Surprise attack, for sure," is all Lapin can tell them. He does not look disappointed. But he says to Cal: "Them Kentucks is good bush-fighters, I'm told. We gotta keep our eyes peeled."

The Pottawatomie are now everywhere. Their yelps and war-cries sail eerily into the clear, perfectly calm air. "Some surprise," Lapin says.

It is only after Cal has checked Papa's musket (he refused the Brown Bess that Lapin offered) several times and tried unsuccessfully to staunch his disappointment that he glances up at the bare-bones tree around him with the dying sun salient upon them that Cal notices the wizened, flesh-red, unfallen fruit they still bear. They're in an orchard. These are apple trees.

Cal excuses himself and slips into the woodlot behind their position. He squats, gets up and eases along what is unquestionably a path. Soon he sees what he has come for: the settler's cottage. Split-log, shingled roof, fieldstone chimney, decades-old. A dozen hutches and coops cozy in the snow. Only the bloodied feathers scattered about the charred foundation of what was once a capacious barn indicated the ravagement that must have occurred here. Cal then notes the smashed windows, the door on one hinge. Nothing on this acre breathes. Frenchtown. Cal shudders.

Among the squads of sappers, gunners and infantrymen that bustle by in the snow-lit dark, Cal cannot help but see the others: trudging, stooped, unacknowledging, freighted with what has been dearly salvaged, their accents in the rare exchanges unmistakable: Maman's tongue. These are the refugees. Choosing a side.

When Cal is woken it is still dark. The road is full of furtive movement. A horse's whinny is a trumpet-blast in the hushed gesturing: the troops jump in unison. In minutes the road is quiet again. A pink blush is showing above the frozen Lake. Cal takes it as a sign: of perpetual humiliation. They wait. They are cold: with no warming fires, no telltale smoke. So close and yet so far. When the assault begins they hear the opening cannonade; the ground under them trembles. Their whoop is half-hearted. A mile away the British musket-fire is distinct, volleyed, and disciplined. Then it breaks up: erratic, prolonged, febrile. Cal sweats and shivers. Nothing will come down this road. The woods behind them is hip-deep with snow; they do not even bother to watch it.

Whistling, Lapin gets a fire going. Boils tea. Makes brisk forays up and down the road. Chats amiably with the cooks and drovers down by the Lake. But everybody comes to attention and listens when the ululations of Roundhead's braves add their own chill to the morning air. Then more cannonfire. It's a battle, this time. Any ground here will be won with blood: for those lucky enough to be among the chosen. Cal burns with shame. He begs whatever gods there be for deliverance. He glares at the bush, willing a Kentuck—bold and lethal and merciless—to materialize out of snow and thicket, like a seven-point stag.

At noon it begins to snow. No wind, just a faithful, repetitious falling that brushed the black branches everywhere.

"Who looted the farms back there?" Cal asks Lapin later with the afternoon fast disappearing and the sounds of the battle winding down, muffled now.

Tonelessly, Lapin says: "We did. That's why we want the town back. To make sure it's burned to ashes."

Cal is puzzled.

"Don't want them Kentucks getting' their toes all toasty an' comfortable over here, now do we?"

Cal remembers the dream he had in the blizzard under the plundered apply trees at Brownstown: moonlight upon the untouchable flesh of his beloved: bone-vulnerable, radiating trust, she cradles his sundering horn with effortless ease and locked in the eldest rhythm they canter to a sweetness of satisfactions and completeness that leaves him weeping, and yes, yes he will make himself worthy, he will repay the lusts of her own craving till all vows dissolve in the mellow aftermath, and moonlight again grips them in its lovers' glow.

Captain Larouche staggers through the snow into full view. His left arm swings loosely as his side. His face is charred with powder-burn.

"It's over, lads," he says to them. "A bloody mess, certain."

Lapin helps him to the fire.

"Roundhead's crew are on the rampage. We're tryin' to get all the wounded, ours an' theirs, back to Brownstown. Take your men up the line about a mile. You'll see a stand of pine. Turn hard right and stay south through the bush. You'll come out onto the Raisin above the main town. Get them wounded Kentucks outta there fast as you can. Bring 'em back along the road. It'll be safer. An' for Chrissake, watch out for the savages. They've gone berserk."

Cal's heart is pumping blood so hard into his head that he can barely see through the swirling flurries. He keeps Lapin in sight. The road ahead is awash with men and horses and hand-drawn sleighs piled with what must be bodies. Whose? The snow blurs all. The shouts and murmurs and groans are clear but they drift disparate and meaningless, flung about in the rising storm. They have won. Further along, Cal trips and almost falls. He is certain his boot struck bone. He peers back. Corporal Jacques is kneeling: brushing away snow furiously. The Corporal reels back, bends over and retches. Cal follows Lapin.

A musket cracks and they all flinch. A drover is heard uttering gargantuan curses, they can now see him beating the dead beast with the butt of a gun. The wood splits. The drover lunges past them. From the stalled cart comes a rattling of moans, all of them human.

"We turn here," Lapin says.

They penetrate deep into the woods. They are following a deer-run, well-packed and meandering. To step off it is to wallow and freeze. The snow has eased off to flurries. It is getting dark. They are lost. But ahead they hear abrupt and strident cries of indeterminable import. They move doggedly, urgently forward, risking the drifts. Through the trees comes a flicker of torchflame. Then: Indian yowls, elongated, full of unappeasable rage. Cal thinks of the wretched encampments, young squaws inviting ravishment, the smell of despair.

"The town's just ahead," Lapin shouts. "Spread out. Make lots of noise. When you find a wounded man or prisoner, take him to the main road, somewhere on our left. Stay put. I'll lead you back."

The dozen who have followed now hesitate. The trek has been exhausting. They haul in lungfuls of air. Fingers are frozen to triggers. No one really knows where he is. No one knows what the enemy looks like. Everyone has a gut-fear of the Pottawatomie.

"Alright men, spread out. Muskets at the ready. Bayonets fixed." Lapin turns to Cal. "Well, you've arrived," he says, and Cal is too surprised to catch the tone of the sergeant's remark. In a second it is too late: Lapin is tramping away through the trees, and is gone.

Corporal Jacques steps away in the other direction. No one else moves. Then, one by one, they take tentative steps towards the garbled human noises getting more vivid and compelling by the moment. Only yards away men are dying. Lapin's men are soldiers. They've been given orders: protect the wounded and the prisoners. But how? Where? To what end? Suddenly courage comes down to the simple business of placing one foot in front of the other.

Cal finds himself alone. He has not budged. The shirt beneath his jackets and sweater is stiff, iced with his sweat. The moustache he has effected is frozen through. His face is aflame. No feeling in either ear. His hand has molded itself to the musket-stock. He can't remember if it is primed and loaded. Or whether the barrel got plugged. If so, he will blow his face apart the second he squeezes the trigger. That thought flits through his mind, but still he does not move.

They are skirmishing all around him, he thinks. Muskets blast or crackle, in no sequence. A howl, a shriek, cries in no discernible language. Ghastly silences, trepid with meaning—for someone. For a short while the silence continues. Cal has no idea how much time has passed. He is chilled to the last hot pit of his bowel, but he is alive. His breathing refuses to cease. The quiet, the gentle fluffing of snow off the tree-limbs, the serenity of night-forests he has worshipped since childhood: these, or something more instinctive inside him, draw him at last into motion.

Somehow he has made it into a sort of clearing. What direction he has come is unknowable. He has kept his mind shut to all sensation, the gun slack at his side. A squaw could have slit his throat with impunity. He has no care. No fear.

He is at the edge of an orchard. The walking has warmed him. He flexes his fingers, peering ahead. A log-barn, torchlight wavering through the blank square of a window. Low voices somewhere inside. He does not approach. He leans against a dwarfed tree. He seems intent on studying the shape of its variegated, antlering, pattern against the sudden presence of deep, star-vivid sky. To the north: gunshots and violent speech erupt and subside. A door flings open, and two scarlet-clad regulars dash out, muskets at the ready, bayonets glittering. They hurl themselves—upright, breasts exposed, eyes on target—towards their duty. Their valour is routine.

Minutes pass. Explosions. Murderous shouting. Valour, death, savagery—but who would bear witness in the snow and the dark at the heart of battle?

From inside the barn comes a chilling shriek, as if a sow were giving breech-birth. Cal's gut clenches, his legs go numb, but nothing can stop his ears. The screams multiply, serrate into howls, it's like a penful of pigs slugged sideways by the sledge and wailing in their pain and in the anticipation of death even as the butcher's blade slices away voice and heart's-blood and all memory of this moment so like the first one beating up that dim fleshy channel to the alienating air.

Out of the open doorway stumbles a figure in blue, hatless, bare feet plunging into snow. Right arm in a sort of sling. Only one leg has any power, the other drags and flops and has to be pulled with the good hand. The hair is thick and blond. It jerks up every time the lame leg strikes the snow, and a wheezing grunt pops out of his mouth. He catches sight of Cal, of the blue jacket, the flintlock. Something like a smile creases his pain. He topples into a drift, not six feet from Cal. Cal stares at him as if he were trying to draw him from memory.

"Help me..." The voice has no connection with this figure, this soldier, this brave pain. It is a child's almost-under-the-ice. Cal knows him. Lapin has mimicked the accent many times: a Kentuck.

The Kentuck lifts himself up and starts to run, the maimed leg pounding into the snow. It is only then that Cal sees the old Wyandot thrashing a few feet behind, with his distinctive feather, his war-paint gleaming with sweat and anticipation. He is panting and lunging and cursing the snow and brandishing a stone-hatchet bigger than his fist.

With a terrible groan the Kentuck tips sideways, his bad leg gone, the pain unendurable. As he does so, his right arm flops out of its sling and sticks up at an angle. A bone glistens. A deep moan rattles through clenched teeth. Then his eyes open wide and he looks straight up into Cal's.

The Wyandot, an aged sachem, flounders towards the Kentuck. He is swollen with rage. He comes like a drowning man through water. The Kentuck raises his arm in supplication or defence and the hatchet cuts right through it and sinks into his chest, below the right shoulder. A whoosh of air comes out of his mouth and he swoons back into the pillowing snow, his eyes jammed open, alert, bracing for pain and whatever might need to be endured. Blood geysers from the wounds, its heat makes a hissing sound as it touches the chill of air and snow.

The Wyandot sees Cal for the first time and pulls out his scalping-knife. The fury in his assassin's glance has not abated. He reaches for the Kentuck's blond hair just as the soldier shrieks at the waves of pain breaking in him. Even in such agony his eyes understand what is happening beyond them: the horror they register is unfathomable.

Something is urging Cal to move: forward, towards the slaughter. The old sachem hears him instantly, pauses, peers over at him. Cal's face tells his story.

The Wyandot then grips the Kentuck's hair menacingly. He shouts a command in his tongue several times: at Cal. Its meaning is plain: shoot him, now. He thrusts the scalping-knife up against the bone, then waits with stony patience. The Kentuck's protests are now gargles of his own blood welling up, but the eyes remain alive, aghast, beseeching.

The sachem turns to see what Cal will do. Something spooks him. His knife flashes. Cal feels the musket flinch in his hands, its concussion rattles through the stiffened trees. The gun drops away. Cal stares at the Kentuck. His eyes are gratefully dead, his scalp intact.

The Wyandot straightens up, then totters backward. His fur vest is ripped open. He puts both hands in the slash to staunch the blood, then sinks forward to his knees, as if praying. The wound puckers and spouts. The eyelids flicker. He has made no sound whatever, no sign of his astonishment.

Cal can no longer put off the inevitable. Without looking down, he brings his right hand up to his stomach. The Wyandot's knife is stuck into something solid there.

Above the apple boughs, the stars are shrinking.

Cal wakes up. The stars have returned, a moon swimming amongst them. Something soft as straw cushions his head. He is moving, he feels the wind slick on his upturned face, the skidding of runners on snow. His head refuses to turn but his eyes slide sideways far enough for him to see that no midnight forest looms beside him, no guiding river-bank. Only emptiness above the snow and ice he is gliding over: stretching off to where it is blessed finally by a single star. He rolls his eyes the other way. Cloth. A sleeve. Blue jacket.

Beneath him, a runner strikes some impediment, lurches, and the sleigh accepts the aftershock. A chord of moans and gasps, some of them do not stop. The jacket next to him is quaking. A voice, a boy's, cries out for its mother, unashamed. Another, wraith-like, chants in monotone: ohgodohgodohgod. The invisible horses gallop steadily, callously towards a far shore. Cal has no galling jabbing pain, nothing that tears apart at each jolt of the sleight. All he feels is a single scalding ache below his stomach, a molten sac of intense, unceasing, unvarying pain that nothing outside his body can penetrate to harm or heal. It is his own. Everywhere else he is numb, all sensation consumed by the fiery centre, and around it, spreading infinitesimally skinward, is a coldness that is not the chill of a winter wind or the freezing of deep snow of the numbing of night-air or Papa's stern unbending face at the bedroom door. Cal does not shiver. His teeth do not chatter, like the wretch beside him. Behind his eyes he can feel a patch of livid warmth just big enough to hold his thought, cruel enough to acknowledge the furnace in his belly and the icy surround that keeps it blazing.

He is certain it was Lapin holding his hand as the Wyandot's knife was jerked, searing, out of his bowel. Cal can't retrieve any of his words, but the sergeant's lips were moving and they would be consoling, fatherly even. He tries to remember what it is he must remember, but there is so little room left in here, a darkness laps at its edges—a friendly soothing sort of darkness where fire and ice can make no sting.

His eyes will not close. They take in the arch of the heavens above them. No horizon mars the stretch and wheel of constellations whose names he knows but can't quite recall (learned by heart on the evening walks when Papa still whistled and assigned a name to each living thing around them and the eternal things above them), and yes, they are still there, they are still beautiful, and yes, Papa, they are still gliding along the indetectable pathways of some vaster journey, you sometimes smiled at their antics in the tales of Crooked Hare, and they are as beautiful as they were when he and Ti-Luc went skating ice-whisked with the Creek under them in the carbon dark of December, and yes they are as beautiful here as when he and Trill—in the June-sweet clover of the First Field—lay dizzying, yards apart as they dropped flat on their angel-backs, bound by secrecy and sharing only the child-wondrous sensation of a star-blazoned sky rolling unbidden and unreined and portentous over a meadow of clover and a world spinning under it like a lunatic top.

Why, you could lie here and marvel at such sights every night for the rest of your life.

When he gets home he will be sure to tell Maman that he has seen the apple tree Cousin Tristesse shook himself out of and, as luck would have it, just missed Bébé Anthyme.

Vision of a lost war at the corner of Innerkip and Ogdensburg

Denis Robillard

It's close to 1 am
The real squalls persist outside
Medics and police attend a wintry scene
Of carnage on the blacktop.
A highway clock blinks 12:48 am
Through a pattern of fluffy bed bug races
Can see bloody shapes laying about in bodily form
Like agonized Pompeii statues.

A numb bomb goes off inside me
Another war fuzzes over me....

Further inside the black bruise of time
I'm back to that first winter 1813
Somewhere on the eastern flange
off the frozen St. Lawrence

Can see a long red column of men
Soldiers, traitors, dupes, heroes—
all class of men suited for hell
Lead by brave MacDonell
they have ice in their veins
crossing Ogdensburg in the dead of winter.

That landscape becomes Birdseye bleak
A painting by Turner of snow over snow
Beyond fatal vision squints

I can imagine a handful of dead Brits on the lake
Strewn to the four winds like some forgotten vow.
Slate gray clouds scour the sky
Of that rigid February air
Can see a column of slanty Grimm stickmen—
"Bent upon chastising the personal insolence he had received"

McDonell's column is rising to meet Forsyth's singular fiery tongue—
And wrench it from his taunting mouth for good.

They obey the wind's harsh curves
Marching headlong into it
Traversing in a petty pace
They seem like awkward fence pieces
Mangled hieroglyphs kneeling
Into obstinacy.
They forge ahead as one willed movement
A horse plow exerted into slow slow snow
The American men fade off into blindness
shot on the spot.
See nothing but a vanishing point of mitered heads
Above this blurred out line bobbing away
Like a slight pin prick of a camera obscura
Marching then falling like rag bags into that cold chill
Canadian wind.

And now with history's blunted mallet
I use the cold conscious chisel of my mind
To wake these abstinent Americans from their icy sleep.

Note on text:

MacDonell wished to remove this threat and proposed to visiting Governor Sir George Prevost on February 21 that an attack be made across the frozen St. Lawrence. Not wishing to draw attention to vulnerability of his supply line, Prevost turned down MacDonnell's plan but allowed him to make a "demonstration" on the ice in front of Prescott across from Ogdensburg.

But to MacDonell the expulsion of Forsyth had become personal. Under a flag of truce, MacDonell had been sent two days earlier to see Forsyth to complain about the unmilitary-like and "predatory" raids on Canadian villages. Forsyth met him only with insults. Later MacDonell admitted that he was "bent upon chastising the personal insolence he had...received from the American Commander."

In the ensuing battle a large part of the town of Ogdensburg was damaged with Forsyth escaping with part of his riflemen overland to Sacket's Harbour. With his sword in the woun of the enemy, and bullet holes in his hat and coat, Forsyth was determined to take back Ogdensburg and requested troops from the officer in command at Sacket's Harbour. But none were forthcoming. Instead of blaming the British, local and military officials placed blame for the attack on Ogdensburg squarely on Forsyth for "his known zeal for a small partisan warfare." Civil leaders in Ogdensburg became hostile to any US troops being stationed in their town again. It was not until October 1813 did US troops finally return to the area. Without federal troops around, a number of the town's citizens took up selling food and supplies to the British troops across the river, a trade that continued throughout the rest of the war.

A Strike Northward: The United States Attacks British North America in the War of 1812

Raymond Souster & Les Green

Brigadier-General Zebulon Montgomery Pike
United States Army

The year 1813 was an eventful one for me,
as I was promoted from colonel to brigadier general.
Washington was well aware that I had
previous experience in frontier campaigns,
so it came as no great surprise to me
that the War Department gave me the task
of mounting an attack on the Lake Ontario town of York,
the enemy capital of Upper Canada. Impatiently I waited
for the break-up of the ice in Sacket's Harbour
where I'd assembled an assault force of six vessels.
U.S. Navy Commodore Isaac Chauncey had assured me
that a surprise attack with the intention of capturing
the newly-built 38 gun British frigate *Sir Isaac Brock,*
along with several smaller ships, would effectively give us
control of the Great Lakes and go a long way
toward our goal of driving the British out of North America.

Accordingly, as planned, our little fleet left Sacket's Harbour
on the 25th of April. After a rough passage
on the flagship USS Madison, we anchored just west
of York on the 26th. At daybreak I gave the command
to launch our long boats and watched as our gallant rifle corps
rowed towards shore. As they neared the beach,
shots were exchanged. Our men replied to the fire

of what turned out to be a band of Indians.
It was at this point that I was unable to restrain myself
from shouting out, "By God, I can't stand here any longer.
Come on, jump into this boat with me." With that,, I urged my officers
to press on and join in the fray. This we did,
and within minutes, were joining our forces in the woods,
first routing the Indians, and then the red-coated
British Grenadiers. It was obvious to me that their troops
expected to engage in the European open style of battle,
apparently having no stomach for a fight in the depths
of the wood. At this juncture we were greatly aided
by a deadly hail of grape shot from our ships' guns.
The way was now clear for our spirited boys
to march towards their fortifications, our fife and drum band
playing "Yankee Doodle". To me it seemed
that victory was now easily within our grasp.

Fate, however, had other plans in store for us
that day. Their General Sheaffe must have made
the early decision that he couldn't defend the town
or save the new ships being built at the harbour front.
Accordingly, he must have given orders to blow up
their main magazine within the fort that formed
their principal defences. We on the other hand
had pressed on to capture two artillery batteries
well within sight of their Government House.

With no warning whatsoever, the ground shook under us
like an earthquake, as all hell broke loose. With a roar
shattering our eardrums and a flash blinding our sight,
a horrendous explosion which must have been caused
by hundreds of barrels of gunpowder rocked the heavens,
catching us beneath a terrifying shower of falling rocks, earth,

and who knows what other debris. And suddenly
I was struck in the spine with what could only have been
part of a huge rock, falling immediately in agony
and remembering little or nothing from then on.

Sometime later I must have regained consciousness,
hearing the groans of wounded and dying men
scattered all around me. In great pain
I somehow managed to lift myself up
and exclaim in my failing voice,
"Push on, my brave fellows,
and avenge your general".
Then I must have lost consciousness again,
to be awakened by a sudden burst of cheering.
An officer kneeling beside me explained
that the Union Jack had been lowered over the fort
and the Stars and Stripes raised in its place.

All I remember after that is awakening in my cabin
aboard ship, knowing full well that death
hovered near to end my pain.

The Author as Amateur Historian

With all resistance ended, the victorious Americans
amid the confusion were allowed to loot and burn
the town. They would remain among the ruins of York
for another six days before sailing away. This proved
to be a hollow victory, for as well as losing their commander,
they had failed in their main objective to capture
the ships under construction, these having been burned
by the British or simply sailed away to safety.

Major General Henry Dearborn
United States Army Northeast Sector

Following the death of our brave comrade General Zebulon Pike,
I assumed command of our invading forces poised to make
yet another assault on the British colony of Upper Canada.
I was well aware that with the destruction of the capital,
the British regular forces in York had been withdrawn to Kingston
on the eastern end of Lake Ontario, thus giving us
a decided advantage in any attack we might choose to make.

With this in mind I wasted no time in transporting my forces
to our Fort Niagara on the eastern bank of the Niagara River,
directly opposite the British Fort George. By May 8 our troops
had arrived from York and on May 25 we commenced hostilities
using the newly-developed invention called heated shot.
This involved cannon balls being heated red hot.
Thus armed, we began a fierce bombardment
of the wooden buildings of Fort George. At the same time
Commodore Chauncey's ships added their fire power and as a result
the British fort soon burned to the ground with their forces
hastily seeking whatever cover was available
and bracing for certain attack. For our part
we received only slight damage to Fort Niagara.

Thus encouraged, but plagued by a painful leg wound,
I turned command over to by my adjutant general,
Winfield Scott. I instructed him to launch an attack on Fort George
from the Lake Ontario side, rather than from across the Niagara River
or from the south. As I had hoped, this thrust coming as it did
from our small fleet carrying 5000 of our men,
landed with only minor resistance at the place
known as Two Mile Creek. The vastly inferior British force

now was compelled to quickly retreat westwards,
thus leaving the whole Niagara peninsula virtually undefended.

The Author as Amateur Historian

This seems perhaps the right moment to introduce
the historic records of Major John Norton, a mixed-blood
war chief of the Mohawk Nation. Coming from Scottish
and Iroquois-Cherokee parentage, he was in the unique position
of being accepted by both the British and the Grand River
Six Nations Community. His absorbingly detailed journals
give us perhaps the most colourful panoramic record
of events in the Niagara campaigns. Together with the simple
but heart-warming account of a self-appointed scout,
the nineteen-year-old United Empire Loyalist descendent Billy Green,
we have an illuminating picture from both the settler
and native sides in this conflict.

Major John Norton
War Chief of the Mohawk Nation

Together with sixty or seventy of my brave Grand Valley warriors,
I was hidden in a wood close by a beach on Lake Ontario,
between the Two Mile Run and Mississagi Point,
west of the ruins of Fort George. Early on that fog bound morning of May 26,
we heard muffled voices somewhere out on the lake,
followed almost immediately by opening rounds of cannon fire
from the enemy's Fort Niagara. This triggered
an intense cannonade from what had to be a sizeable fleet
anchored offshore. After an hour of intense gunfire
which seemed to terrify all our defenders,
and meeting little or no resistance the enemy troops
swarmed ashore. My British allies, easily outnumbered by ten to one,

made one suicidal attack before wisely retreating
to regroup their forces. The British plan now appeared to be
to gradually retreat westward along the peninsula
toward the comparative safety of Burlington Heights,
where if they were reinforced by Six Nations warriors and local militia,
a determined stand could be made.

For some puzzling reason, the Americans seemed to have
no appetite to follow up their early successes,
and on the 27 and 28 of May our retreat continued
unmolested to Forty Mile Creek. Here I was encouraged
that Brigadier General John Vincent had decided
that this place, being easily defensible,
would give us a much-needed breathing space, before continuing
the retreat to our final destination.

Brigadier-General John Chandler
United States Army

On the morning of June 5, I arrived at Forty Mile Creek.
The detachment under our General Winder then had
marching orders for Stoney Creek. After a short halt,
our combined forces struck out for that objective. Arriving there
at between five and six o'clock we found a small British picket in place
which retired hastily on our approach. Our advance guard pursued
and soon fell in with a more formidable enemy picket
of about one hundred strong under their Colonel Williams.
A brisk skirmish ensued. While I hastened to the main body,
Williams retreated and our advance followed in pursuit.
This chase lasted longer than I could have wished,
with the advance guard rejoining our troops just at sunset.

I ordered our 13th and 14th Regiments, who were in the rear,
to take a position for the night near the mouth of the creek
to cover our supply boats should they arrive. A favourable position
presenting itself, I encamped with the residue of our troops
where we halted, placing an advance picket
from half to three-quarters of a mile in front, expressly ordering them
to maintain a constant patrol. I gave positive orders for the troops
to lay on their arms. Contrary to my orders, fires were kindled.
But there are doubts whether in the long run this worked for or against us.

I did anticipate the enemy might attack us that night
if he intended to fight, but perhaps this was not expected
by all. I had my horse confined near me and directed as well
that the harnesses should not be taken from the horses of the artillery.

Lieutenant James Fitzgibbon
British Army Regular

To determine the exact location of the American lines
at Stoney Creek, I came up with a crazy
but well-thought-out plan that would reveal any secrets
the American army might be attempting to hide.
I dressed up as a peddler pretending to sell butter
and to my amazement was able to walk around
the whole of the enemy's camp unchallenged.
The nearby Gage's farmstead had been taken over
for the comfort of the American officers,
with the family being securely locked
in the basement. There were soldiers guarding
everything in sight whether or not it was important.
When I returned safely to our camp at Burlington Heights,
I knew every single detail about the battle plans
the Americans had in mind.

Billy Green, Scout
Son of United Empire Loyalist Settlers

Remarkably, I was the first white child born at Stoney Creek,
this happening on February 4, 1794. At the time
of the Battle of Stoney Creek I was 19 years old,
my home still being in that place. About 6 o'clock
on the morning of June 5, 1813, we heard
that the American Army were camping below the Forty Mile Creek,
so my brother Levi and I went along the road on top
of the mountain. We got to the Forty, looking down on the creek
until noon, when we saw enemy troops marching up the road.
We stayed there until all but a few of the enemy had passed
through the Village. Then we gave loud war whoops.
I tell you those simple fellows did run!

After that we rushed down the mountain to the road which the Americans
had just passed by on. Brother Levi came across a soldier
with his boot off wrapping a rag around his foot. The soldier
grabbed for his gun, but Levi was too quick for him,
hitting him with a stick until he cried out in pain
causing some of their scouts to open fire on us.

With their shots wildly missing us, we scrambled back up
to the top of the mountain. I started whooping again,
with Levi responding in kind, all this done
in the hope of giving those Yanks a real good scare. By this time
the settlers had come out to the brow of the mountain
to see what all the fuss was about. We waved to them
as we continued down the slope to brother Levi's place nearby.
When we heard the enemy coming through our village
of Stoney Creek down below, curiosity made us come out
to see where they were headed. Some of them spotted us,
then fired on us, almost hitting Levi's girl Hannah.

My next move was to seek out Isaac Corman at his house
not too far away. Once there, I gave a whistle,
which brought out my sister Keziah, Corman's wife. On questioning,
she managed to blurt out that the enemy had taken him prisoner,
leading him down toward the beach. Alarmed by her words,
I started at once and ran, every now and then stopping and whistling
until I crossed the creek. When to my great relief
I heard Isaac's unmistakable hoot like an owl nearby,
I figured he was in enemy hands, but to my great surprise
I made him out approaching me all alone. When I asked
how he'd broken loose, he laughingly told me,
"Their major and I got to talking and he said he was second cousin
to General Harrison. I did him one better by answering
that I was Harrison's first cousin, with my family
coming from Kentucky. Not long after that
a message came for the major. I could scarcely believe my ears
when he told me, "I must leave you now, you're free to go Corman".
When I asked how I could make my way through the lines,
to my surprise the major quickly gave me the enemy countersign.

After I'd received it, I decided at once
to head for the British forces some distance away
at Burlington Heights. I went up the hill to Levi's house
and borrowed his old horse Tip. My next move
was to ride at a gallop until Tip made it clear
that he could go no further. Dismounting, I tied old Tip
to a fence post and hurried the rest of the way on foot
to the British camp.

Arriving there I was at first taken for a spy and underwent
some tough questioning. It wasn't until I'd told my entire story
and revealed the countersign, that I was totally believed.

Then I explained to my questioner, Colonel Harvey,
to the best of my knowledge, where and how the American army
were encamped near Stoney Creek. After the Colonel
apparently had a short exchange with General Vincent,
the decision was made to start at once for Stoney Creek
and they commenced to get things underway. Our forces
began the march at about 11:30 p.m. When asked by Colonel Harvey
if I knew the way through the total darkness, I replied,
"Yes, every inch of it". With that I was given
a corporal's sword and ordered to take the lead.

At times during the march I would get way ahead of the rest
and had to go back to hurry them up, telling them
it would be daylight before we arrived
if we didn't pick up the pace. In reply someone remarked
we would die soon enough. At one point three Yankee sentries
fired at us and then disappeared. This made us
much more cautious. Not long after I spotted an enemy sentry
carelessly leaning against a tree. I told the man behind me
to shoot him, but Colonel Harvey said, "No, run him through".
And he was quickly dispatched. The next sentry we met up with
was at the local church. Before he could load his old gun,
I grabbed it with one hand and put my sword to him with the other.

Lieutenant-Colonel Harvey
Second-in-command to Brigadier-General Vincent

A boy named Billy Green came to me saying thtat
he knew the password for the Americans.
(Wil-Hen-Har, short for William Henry Harrison, the American general).
The problem was that we were outnumbered three to one,
our ammunition was running low and the Americans

controlled the lake. A surprise night attack seemed the only way
for us to establish victory over the Yankees.

After a hurried meeting with General Vincent,
the decision was made to take 704 men
from the 8th and 49th Regiments at Burlington Heights
and force-march them through the night
to attack the estimated 3500 American soldiers.

Here we were lucky in having a scout in the person
of young Billy Green who knew the mountain paths
like no one else could. Stopping just short of the American lines,
we formed into sections and put down the charges
from our muskets, so as not to warn the American enemy
if one should be accidentally discharged.Then we continued our march
quietly and cautiously. Encountering two sentries
we promptly ran them through, but a third managed
to fire his musket, thus no doubt alerting the enemy
to our approach. Immediately I gave the order
for my soldiers to form a line of battle. Now boldly marching
on either side of the road, we moved straight ahead.

Billy Green The Scout
Son of United Empire Loyalist Settlers

Soon we could make out their camp fires.
The order was given to fix flint and fire'
We fired three rounds and advanced about one hundred yards.
Then we reloaded and banged away again.
There was a rush toward our middle rank.
Their south flank charged us. Next came orders
for our flank to charge. This is where we lost

most of our men. Our centre rank captured two of their guns.
The general order was given to charge
and we drove them back and could hear them
scampering wildly through the darkness. Then came the order
to fire again and we shot all our powder away.
With the arrival of daylight, we could see the enemy
continuing to retreat in all directions. Major Plenderleath,
with thirty men of the 49th, and Major Ogilvie
with the 8th or King's Regiment charged and captured
four field pieces in very gallant style. American Generals Chandler
and Winder were captured near their cannon. Our General Vincent
following close behind the rear of his army
somehow managed to get lost in the dark foggy night
in the bushes. He was found in the morning after the battle,
seemingly distressed at losing his hat. To sum up, eighty of our good men
were killed with one hundred and fifty wounded.
We found out later that our enemy had suffered two hundred killed
and two hundred and forty wounded.

Brigadier-General John Chandler
United States Army

Still with my forces in their old position, I heard the alarm
about an hour before daylight on June 6. I was instantly up,
and the forces lying nearby were almost as instantly formed,
as were those under the immediate eye of General Winder.
Our advance pickets having failed us, we were not aware
of the British advance until they were within five hundred yards
of our line. The extreme darkness prevented us
from seeing or knowing at what point they intended to attack us
until their thrust was made upon our right.

My troops responded with a well-directed fire
from nearly the whole line. This, however,
didn't seem to affect the enemy to any great extent,
as I now heard shouts and the din of battle
coming from all directions. I quickly decided I had no choice
but to restore a sense of order to my forces
and to do this, I rode at full speed to the right
to prevent my flank from being turned.
I had barely begun to ride off at a gallop
when without any warning my horse collapsed under me,
resulting in my receiving a serious injury. Wincing at every step
from the terrible pain, I made my way in the darkness to the right,
finally finding Major Smith to whom I gave emergency orders.

While returning to the centre of the line
where our artillery was stationed, I was unlucky enough
to be taken prisoner by the enemy. Thus totally removed
from the battle, I could only hope that General Winder
would somehow rally our battered forces.
To my utter mortification, I was soon informed that he too
had suffered the same fate as I,
ending up a humiliated British captive.

Lieutenant Colonel Harvey
Second-in-command to Brigadier-General Vincent

The grim battle continued in every corner of the night
with the most terrible shouts and shrieks
creating sheer bedlam. Not long after, I learned
that many American soldiers were retreating from their camp,
with others attempting to escape towards the higher ground to the south,
leaving behind their blankets, knapsacks and muskets.

We were then forced to halt to reload our muskets.
Taking advantage of this, the remaining Americans
poured a withering fire upon us, killing many
of our brave men. Despite the chaos and confusion,
our soldiers quickly reformed and sensing victory near at hand
began to charge the enemy. A rout quickly followed
with the Americans retreating towards Forty Mile Creek,
battered tails between their legs. Thus the Battle of Stoney Creek
ended with a bitter, hard-won victory.

The Author Aas Amateur Historian

With this battle over, the Americans realized that their dream
of capturing the Niagara peninsula, the road to Kingston,
and the St. Lawrence valley, had finally died. Peace was at last restored
with the Treaty of Ghent in 1815. But still in 1866 the Fenian Brotherhood
of America would make several last futile attempts across the border
to conquer British North America. This threat of conquest forced the
politicians into the adoption of a federal union
of the four existing British colonies namely, Upper and Lower Canada,
New Brunswick and Nova Scotia. And so on July 1, 1867
the Dominion of Canada was born.

Thus due to the heroic efforts of such diverse men
as Sir Isaac Brock, Chief Tecumseh, John Norton,
John Harvey and Billy Green the seeds were sown
for an independent nation north of the 49th parallel.

98

A Measure of Powder

Keith Inman

The earth exploded.
Her ears rang. An obtuse light
fractured the room. The kitchen.
She was in the kitchen.
Feet on a table. Head
on the boards. The roof tilted
at an odd angle. She stumbled
through the door. Men screamed. Fire
lit her face. "What in he..." The
wall was a tumbled smash
of timber, a torso and a Private's
hat. Blood drained
onto the steaming ground.
She ran across the courtyard.
Grape shot crackled. Smoke rose
from the south rise. Shrill voices
echoed between buildings.
A Captain grabbed her arm.
"There's been four direct hits. Ma'am,
please, take yourself to the infirmary."
"The Magazine's on fire!"
"Are you positive, Ma'am."
"Measure your shot, young sir!"
"Aid the infirm, ma'am." The boy
saluted, and turned toward the smoke.
The infirmary door stood ajar.
Something, like a pile of clothes,
blocked it. She pushed hard,
and the pooling darkness revealed itself
in its bloodied white shift.

An Ode to the High Park Grenadier

Bianca Lakoseljac

Inspired by the myth of a British Grenadier who was believed to have fallen through the ice during the War of 1812 and was never found. Legend has it that Grenadier Pond is bottomless. Some park visitors have claimed that they felt watched from below while canoeing on the pond. Others reported that they felt eyes observing them from below the ice of the frozen pond. The pond has been a popular canoeing and skating place for Torontonians since the park was donated to the city in the late eighteen hundreds.

You are not there,
I said.

An embodiment of my primal self
incarnated want
failed aspirations
longing craving ache
is in your eyes
in mine.

Deep and green is
your subterranean womb
of muddy peaks.

Your eyes are mine
bejeweled in oak leaves.

Yes,
I said
and followed you
hand in hand.

“A Grenadier I am
entombed in an icy scab
and if you scratch your corneal guard
and peer through my sodden skies

your vision
mine
your eternal botched self
mine mine mine.

The war of 1812
the Battle of Fort York
I a Grenadier of the King’s 8th
regiment
plunged to my throne of incarnated want
failed aspirations
longing craving ache.

Your stomping grounds
your dog-walking trails
your lovers’ stroll
willow crowns luminous in icy rain
swaying in their mint overcoats.

I gaze
through silken moonlight
from the muddy depths
of my sleeping eyes.

Give me your hand
my forlorn bride
and I will be your eternal lover

—a soldier of your
incarnated want
failed aspirations
longing craving ache."

A shroud of snowflakes
we stand on guard
hand in hand
my Grenadier and I
gazing
through silken moonlight.

Look down
into murky depths
of our sodden skies.
We're there
eternally.

—Skaters on thin ice
paddles rippling along the corneas of our sleeping eyes—

his eyes mine...

Scene Sixth—Tecumseh's Part of the Field

excerpt from *Tecumseh, a Drama*

Charles Mair

Enter TECUMSEH

TECUMSEH:
This is our summer—when the painted wilds,
Like pictures in a dream, enchant the sight.
The forest bursts in glory like a flame!
Its leaves are sparks; its mystic breath the haze
Which blends in purple incense with the air.
The Spirit of the Woods had decked his home,
And put his wonders like a garment on,
To flash, and glow, and dull, and fade, and die.
Oh, let not manhood fade within my soul!
And thou, pale doubt, that hast distracted me—
Ye forecasts that would drag my spirit down—
Hence and forever flee! Ye have no place,
No business in this breast. My field is here!
Here must my people's cause be lifted up,
Or sink to rise no more.
[Exit]

Enter three American SCOUTS, looking cautiously about them,

1st SCOUT:
This is their spot.

2nd SCOUT:
I see them coming. Look! away—away—
[Exeunt]

(Firing, and other sounds of conflict are heard from PROCTOR'S part of the field, and then suddenly stop.
Re-enter TECUMSEH, with STAYETA and his other Chiefs and Warriors)

STAYETA:
The noise of battle rose, and then it ceased
Almost upon beginning. This is strange.

TECUMSEH:
It is; ah, Proctor, how my soul mistrusts thee!
Go, some of you, see what this silence means—
But stay—here comes a witness of the fight.

Enter LEFROY, out of breath, and excited.

LEFROY:
The line was broken by a charge of horse,
And, in the British quarter, all is lost.

TECUMSEH:
And Proctor—he who meant to leave his bones,
If so God willed it—

LEFROY:
Willed it otherwise!
Upon the instant of attack he fled;
And, seeing this, the line gave way at once.

TECUMSEH:
'Twas this I feared. He loves his wretched life
Too well to leave his vile bones anywhere.
Dastard and coward! Oh, the heavens should crack,

And dart their lighting down upon this slave!
How come such creatures 'mongst the breed of men
To make their nation blush?

LEFROY:
I cannot tell.
Like sulphur in rain-channels after storms,
Or little frogs, one marvels how they come.
But some fought well; Baby, among the rest,
Who is now prisoner. Myself was saved
Most strangely by a boy—a youthful brave,
Whose arrows helped me in a dangerous spot.
I never saw so sweet a lad before.
His face! I started when I saw it first—
It seemed so like to Iena's! Think you,
Could she be here?

TECUMSEH:
Impossible!

DACHOTA CHIEF:
No, no.
'Twas Chaska, of our nation; one who longs
For plumes before his time. He has been seen.
Yet is so active that we cannot catch him.

LEFROY:
Ah, then, 'twas he! This way he ran before me,
Round the rough angle of the lower swamp,
Then darted into it. I followed fast,
And sought, but could not find him—he was gone.

(A flourish of trumpets without, sounding the advance of the American Force)

SAYETA:
Hark! Now the Long-Knives come!

TECUMSEH:
Yes, now they come.
Courage! Warriors, courage! Let our deeds
Take colour from the scene. Now we must fight
Like men; not run like slaves. What matters it
To those who fled, and left us, if they flee?
They can join palms, make peace, draw treaties up,
And son and father, reconciled again,
Will clap their hands, and glory in their race
Which hath despoiled our own. For us, no peace
Save what our axes gain, or, in our graves.
Therefore—as men fore-doomed to war or death—
Let valour make excuse that we shall live
And, breathing vengeance, shake our spoilers so
That they will reel in terror to the East,
From whence they came and cry—"The West is yours!"
Oh, warriors, think of all, and strike like me
Whose homes are in their hands, whose souls are free.
The voice that calls you now will call no more,
For something whispers to this fearless heart—
Here must I fight, and for my people die!

DELAWARE CHIEF:
Then shall we fight and die with you like men.

DACHOTA CHIEF:
Or live to see you Chief of all our race.
(A flourish without, then enter the American Forces. A fierce hand-to-hand conflict begins)

TECUMSEH:
Our foes are turning! Strike them! beat them back!

STAYETA:
Pursue! pursue!

(The American Troops retreat fighting. Exeunt omnes)
Enter IENA from behind

IENA:
I hear, yet cannot see
The dreadful fray! My arrows are all spent.
There are a thousand in my quivered heart
Could I but match them to this useless bow.
What shall I do? Ah, this is our own tree!
It will protect me whilst I wait the end.

[Retires behind a large sugar maple.
Re-enter a small band of Braves, driven back by Soldiers, who chase them out and then return.]

1st SOLDIER:
Ha, ha, those red-skins fled like hunted wolves!
Away, and start another pack!
[Exeunt forward]

IENA:
[looking out] Alas!
Our people 'gin to flee—I fear—I fear,
Here comes my love! Oh, for one arrow more!

Enter LEFROY and an AMERICAN OFFICER fighting with swords In the struggle they draw abreast of IENA's tree and pause.

OFFICER:
You are a white man.

LEFROY:
I am a white man.

OFFICER:
And what a soulless one are you who leave
Your place in civil, good society
To herd with savages; from one extreme
Falling away unto the basest side—
The furthest from the humanizèd world.

LEFROY:
Nay, I deny it! Further, I would say,
My genius leans, like Nature, to all sides,
Can love them all at once, and live with all.

OFFICER:
So! so! you are a poet, painter, what?
Well, that is nothing; I must try and kill you.
[They fight again, and LEFROY disarms the OFFICER]

LEFROY:
Now might I kill you if I had the heart.
Be prisoner instead; I cannot kill
A man thus, in cold blood.
Re-enter two SOLDIERS

OFFICER:
'Tis more than kind.

1st SOLDIER:
Why, that's our captain there, disarmed—let fly!
My carbine is unloaded.

(Second SOLDIER aims at LEFROY. IENA, with a cry, leaps from her shelter and intercepts the shot)

LEFROY:
Who is this?
Not Chaska! Oh no, no,—'tis Iena!
I see her now, who could not see my love—
Love clear and incorruptible as glass,
Love that had dared a monster, wilds and floods—
Dare fire, and draw the bow that shielded me.
Speak to me Iena! No voice—she's dead!

OFFICER:
This is the strangest chapter of my life—
Soldiers, stand off, and rest upon your arms.

LEFROY:
Silent for ever! Oh, my girl! my girl!
Those rich eyes melt; those lips are sun-warm still—

They look like life, yet have no semblant voice.
Millions of creatures throng, and multitudes
Of heartless beings flaunt upon the earth:
There's room enough for them; but thou, dull Fate—
Thou cold and partial tender of life's field,
That pluck'st the flower, and leav-st the weed to thrive—
Thou hadst not room for her! Oh, I must seek
A way out of the rack—I need not live.

OFFICER:
The world grows less familiar every hour:—
Is that a girl?

LEFROY:
Yes, yes, but she is dead—
And love is left upon the earth to starve.
My object's gone, and I am but a shell,
A husk, an empty case, or anything
That may be kicked about the world.
[Exit LEFROY carrying IENA]

OFFICER:
I see!
I have a tear or two behind these eyes,
And they are coming. If he need a friend
I know of one.

2nd SOLDIER:
Now, dang me, who'd 'a thought
That was a girl!

OFFICER:
(Turning aside) What strange and selfless paths
Do skirt the world's hard highway! I have seen
What gives me sight. The tide of battle rolls
Back, and our people win, as win they must:
But, now, methinks, I'll strive with different heart.
Come, soldiers, let's away and join the fight.
[Exeunt through a by-entrance]

Re-enter TECUMSEH's warriors driven back, and then re-enter TECUMSEH, STAYETA, and other Chiefs

TECUMSEH:
Has death died out, that no one now can die?
Or are you driven back by fear of it?
Oh, slaves or men, determine which you are!

Re-enter the American troops, in pursuit

STAYETA:
Tecumseh, calls! On, warriors, strike them down!

(TECUMSEH and his warriors, by a fierce onslaught, again drive their opponents back. The fight continues without—then re-enter TECUMSEH mortally wounded.)

TECUMSEH:
Great Spirit, hadst thou spared me but one hour—
Yet thy behest rules all.

Re-enter DELAWARE CHIEF, also wounded

DELAWARE CHIEF:
What! wounded too?

TECUMSEH:
Yes, I am shot. Recall some warriors
To bear my body hence. Give no alarm,
Lest our poor braves lose courage; but make haste—
I have not long to live. Yet hear my words!
Bury me in the deep and densest forest,
And let no white man know where I am laid.
Promise this ere you go.

DELAWARE CHIEF:
I promise it.
Alas, alas, our bravest and our best!
[Exit DELAWARE CHIEF]

TECUMSEH:
The hour is come! these weary hands and feet
Draw to the grave. Oh, I have loved my life,
Not for my own but for my people's cause.
Who now will knit them? who will lead them on?
Lost! lost! lost! The pale destroyer triumphs!
I see my people flee—I hear their shrieks—
And none to shield or save! My axe! my axe!—
Ha—it is here! No, no—the power is past.
O Mighty Spirit, shelter—save—my people!
[Dies]

Tecumseh's Death

Major John Richardson

Amid that scene, like some dark towering fiend,
    With death-black eyes and hands all spotted o-er,
The fierce Tecumseh on his tall lance leaned,
    Fired with much spoil and drunk with human gore;
And now his blasting glance ferocious gleamed—
    The chief who leads the eagles to his shore—
When, with one scream that devils might appal,
Deep in his breast he lodged the whizzing ball.

Like the quick bolt that follows on the flash
    Which rends the mountain oak in fearful twain,
So swings the warrior with internal dash
    Upon the Christian writhing in his pain;
High gleamed his hatchet, ready now to crash
    Along the fibres of his swimming brain,
When from the adverse arm a bullet flew
With force resistless, and with aim too true.

The baffled Chieftan tottered, sunk, and fell,
    Rage in his heart, and vengeance in his glance;
His features ghastly pale—his breast was hell;
    One bound he made to seize his fallen lance,
But quick the death-shades o'er his vision swell,
    His arms dropped nerveless, straining to advance;
Once look of hated, and the last, he gave,
Then sunk and slumbered with the fallen brave.

Forth from the copse a hundred foemen spring,
    And pounce like vultures on the bleeding clay;
Like famished bloodhounds to the corse they cling,
    And bear the fallen hero's spoils away;
The very covering from his nerves they wring,
    And gash his form, and glut them o'er their prey,—
Wild hell-fiends all, and revelling at his death,
With bursting shrieks and pestilential breath.

Death of Tecumseh

excerpt from *The Canadian Brothers*
Major John Richardson

It was with a sparkling eye and a glowing check that, just as the English troops had halted to give unequal battle to their pursuers, Tecumseh passed along the line, expressing in animated language the delight he felt at the forthcoming struggle, and when he had shaken hands with most of the officers (we fancy we can feel the generous pressure of his fingers even at this remote period) he moved into the dense forest where his faithful bands were lying concealed, with a bounding step that proved not only how much his heart had been set upon the cast, but how completely he confided in the result. And who shall say what that result might not have been even notwithstanding the discomfiture of the English had the heroic Chieftan been spared to his devoted country! But this was not fated to be. Early in the action he fell by the hand of a distinguished leader of the enemy, and his death carried, as it could not fail to do, the deepest sorrow and dismay into the hearts of his followers, who with a spirit that proved their desire to avenge the loss of their noble leader, it was evident, wanted the directing genius of him they mourned to sustain them in the effort. For several days after the action did they continue to hang upon the American rear, as the army again retired with its prisoners upon Detroit; but each day their attack became feebler and feebler, announcing that their numbers were fast dispersing into the trackless region from which they had been brought, until finally not a shot was to be heard disturbing the night vigils of the American sentinels.

With the defeat of the British army, and the death of Tecumseh, perished the last hope of the Indians to sustain themselves as a people against the inroads of their oppressors. Dispirited and dismayed, they retired back upon the hunting groups which still remained to them, and there gave way both to the deep grief with which every heart was overwhelmed at the loss of their truly great leader, and to the sad anticipations which the increasing gloom that clouded the horizon of their prospects naturally induced.

TECUMSEH AND THE EAGLES

Bliss Carman

I

TECUMSEH of the Shawnees
He dreamed a noble dream,—
A league to hold their freedom old
And make their peace supreme.

He drew the tribes together
And bound them to maintain
Their sacred pact to stand and act
For common good and gain.

II

The eagles taught Tecumseh
The secret of their clan,—
A way to keep o'er plain and steep
The liberty of Man.

The champions of freedom
They may not weary soon,
Nor lay aside in foolish pride
The vigilance of noon.

Those teachers of Tecumseh
Were up to meet the dawn,
To scan the light and hold the height
Till the last light was gone.

Like specks upon the azure,
Their guards patrolled the sky,
To mount and plane and soar again
And give the warning cry.

They watched for lurking perils,
The death that skulks and crawls,
To take by stealth their only wealth
On wind-swept mountain walls.

They did not trust the shadows
That sleep upon the hill;
Where menace hid, where cunning slid,
They struck—and struck to kill.

Through lonely space unmeasured
They laid their sentry rings,
Till every brood in eyrie rude
Was shadowed by their wings.

Tecumseh watched the eagles
In summer o'er the plain,
And learned their cry, "If freedom die,
Ye will have lived in vain."

III

The vision of Tecumseh
It could not long endure;
He lacked the might to back the right
And make his purpose sure.

Tecumseh and his people
Are gone; they could not hold
Their league for good; their brotherhood
Is but a tale that's told.

IV

The eagles of Tecumseh
Still hold their lofty flight,
And guard their own on outposts lone,
Across the fields of light.

They hold their valiant instinct
And know their right of birth,
The do not cede their pride of breed
For things of little worth.

They see on earth below them,
Where time is but a breath,
Another race brought face to face
With liberty or death.

Above a thousand cities
A new day is unfurled,
And still on high those watchers cry
Their challenge o'er the world.

Where the patriots are marching
And battle flags are borne,
To South and North their cry goes forth
To rally and to warn.

From border unto border,
They wheel and cry again
That master cry, "If freedom die,
Ye will have lived in vain!"

Wm. Henry Harrison's speech on the death of Tecumseh

excerpt from *Tecumseh, A Drama*

Charles Mair

HARRISON:
Sleep well, Tecumseh, in thy unknown grave,
Thou mighty savage, resolute and brave!
Thou, master and strong spirit of the woods,
Unsheltered traveller in sad solitudes,
Yearner o'er Wyandot and Cherokee,
Couldst tell us now what hath been and shall be!
[Exeunt]

Tecumseh/Last Thoughts on the Thames

Don Gutteridge

At last
they have given up
the centuries-long
pursuit of my bones—
grim souveniring
(Indian skin
tanned and braided
in a girl's hair,
my scalp is
leather for some
Yankee museum,
my tongue a
tobacco every
Long-Knife yearns
to chew on,
dip their fingers
in my interminable
blood, whisper
my name over and
over as they lance
the quivering female)

They would not leave
me graveless,
needed this proof
of their courage,
or maybe they
really did know

our bones belong
to the place that
gave them length,
that my name would
survive the cursing
of present voices,
my skeleton hand
like a smoking
question-stroke
over these death-grounds,
over these last
few countries
I now call my
home, my grave

Of course, there is
nothing to find:
my corpse was not
cached in some
animal's burrow,
nor cut up and
broadcast under the
ceremonial moon,

when the bullet
struck my heart
split once like a
milkweed pod
and we floated
myriad and free....

Yet I cannot leave,
that is my burden,

for 160 years
my spirit has found its rest
here in these southern counties
in the last field before Moraviantown.

At first is was much
like my birth-ground:
the Thames (despite an
English name) found
its own way thru the
wooded bottomlands,
easy and effortless it
brought the seasons down
over my thousand bones
and for a while
it might have been the
Wabash   Ohio   Miami....

In the town of Chatham
children play ball
on a green field
which bears my name
(their laughter is a
music I remember:
let me call out—
the game goes on)

And there are streets
and learning-places
inscribed with the
letters of my name,
and I have heard them
strangely on the lips

of school-children
telling of the battle,
of the Chief's bones
hidden beneath a
cellar, a barn-floor,
a forged grave-mark—
and some of them
strangely are sad,
and one too old
for his age
sits in a
cramped room and
draws my name
over and over
'til there's no
more white
on the white

page

Tecumseh's Bones

Marty Gervais

Some say he's buried on Walpole Island. Others claim he's buried in a farmer's field on the other side of Thamesville.

There are those, too, who believe his skull had been preserved at McGill University in Montreal before it was lost in a fire on April 16, 1907.

I'm talking about Tecumseh, the great native leader of the Shawnee and a large tribal confederacy that joined with the British and went to war with the U.S. in 1812.

Windsor historian and former University of Windsor political science professor Trevor Price believes, as do many other historians and folklorists, that Tecumseh's body was dumped into a mass grave along with the fallen at the Battle of Moraviantown Oct. 5, 1813.

And it's true that a farmer many decades ago stumbled upon a collection of bones, and pushed them to one end of his field to move them out of the way, Price pointed out.

"So there's really no way of knowing what's there," he added.

That search for Tecumseh's gravesite, however, is bound to arise in the book he's writing on the life of Tecumseh. It will be one in a series being released later this year by the Essex County Historical Society. The first in this series, published last month with the assistance of an Ontario Trillium grant, is a reprint of the long out-of-print book The Windsor Border Region, written by Rev. E.J. Lajeunesse.

Price, president of the local historical society and author of another book, Heritage Along the Detroit River, said there is wildly conflicting speculation over the death of Tecumseh and what happened to his body after that fateful battle.

Even how Tecumseh died is the subject of disagreement, he said.

Kentuckian rifleman Col. Richard Johnson, who was hit five times in that battle, boasted of having shot the great warrior in the chest when he was attacked by him. Johnson actually didn't immediately take credit for this, but when news reached home that he had single-handedly killed Tecumseh, he became a national hero. Price said it helped Johnson get elected as vice-president in 1837.

William Whitley, a Revolutionary War veteran and companion of Daniel Boone, is also credited with executing Tecumseh.

As a matter-of-fact, the five-foot-five inch flintlock rifle he allegedly used to kill him can be seen at a museum in his honour in Crab Orchard, Ky.

"But there's no conclusive evidence that any of this happened," asserts Price.

As for the location of Tecumseh's body, those stories, too, abound, Price says.

Legend has it that his followers came at night and whisked his body away, and that for years Tecumseh's bones were hidden, and moved several times.

How they came to rest at Walpole Island is based on a story that John Nahdee, who had been with Tecumseh at the time of his death, conveyed the bones of the great Indian chief to Ste. Anne's Island, adjacent to Walpole, and buried them there.

Nahdee himself moved his band to Walpole in 1848 after surrendering some 300 acres of their reserve in Anderdon Township where he had settled after the War of 1812.

The bones eventually were exhumed and moved to Walpole. Or so it has been maintained.

And today a monument sits overtop what is purported to be the grave of Tecumseh.

"I really don't think that's where it is," says Price, who suggests it would be easy enough to determine if the bones could be dug up, and examined.

The Shawnee warrior's great-grandson, Thomas Wildcat Alford, a member of the Absentee Shawnees of Oklahoma, also believes Tecumseh was buried near the battlefield at a site that was later flooded, and all evidence of that grave has been washed away.

More important to Price, however is erecting a statue of Tecumseh, and he suggests Amherstburg is the right place.

"That is where Tecumseh made that rousing speech," Price said, pointing out that in that address at Fort Malden to Maj.-Gen. Henry Procter of the British forces, he rallied the soldiers and his new confederacy of natives to take this war to the U.S.

Tecumseh's last words in that oration were: "You have got the arms and ammunition ... If you have any idea of going away, give them to us and you may go ... For us, our lives are in the hands of the Great Spirit. We are determined to defend our lands, and if it is his will we wish to leave our bones upon them."

What's in a Name? The Pursuit of George Peacock, Namesake of Peacock Point

John B. Lee

Peacock Point does not appear on most maps of the province of Ontario, Canada. Few people have heard of it, and most people would be hard pressed to find it. Go for a Sunday drive in your car along the north shore of Lake Erie between Nanticoke in the West and Selkirk in the East and you barely know that you've passed through it. It is a humble cottage community built on a cliff overlooking the Lake and cast in the three-miles-away shadow of the eight-hundred foot stacks of Nanticoke, the second largest coal-fired electricity generating plant in the world.

The cliffs are high, the beach is stony, and from the lake the projected tip of land looks like an ugly series of abandoned bunkers. These are the breakwalls constructed to combat the erosion that has been eating its way into the precipice at a rate accelerated by the rising water levels of the seventies and eighties. The ruptured gabions, rusty crimped-metal panels, jagged rows of weathered railway ties, rugged heaps of cut stone, and monotonous goose-gray building blocks of cement set together in a precarious jig-saw that climbs from water level to tree line combine to make a most uninviting boater's view of the place. Still despite these efforts to defeat weather and the force of the lake, fissures appear in lawns, trees lose their footing and tilt drunkenly to the south, and wet clay cakes slide and vomit into the surf making a soupy brown wash of the spring shore.

My family and I spend our summers in a cedar cottage on the corner of Lakeshore and Lakeside Drive in Peacock Point. We bought in 1985 and, as always when we first move in to a new community, I became interested in how this place got its name. This is the story of how this small cottage community came to be called "Peacock Point".

In March of 1807 an American blacksmith by the name of George Peacock came to the Niagara district of Upper Canada with his wife and six children in search of land. He would eventually be caught up in the forces which opposed the British in the War of 1812, and his son George Peacock Jr. would be executed for the crime of High Treason at Burlington Heights on July 20th, 1814.

In that he was a man of neither wealth, nor influence, and given the political climate of the day, and his own predicament as a late-come American, George Peacock Sr. had little hope of fulfilling his dream of acquiring land in Upper Canada. Nonetheless, he petitioned the executive council, dated at York, May 16, 1807 for a Crown Lease of Lot 21, Concession Front. "Concession Front" signifies the fact that the land was located on the shore of Lake Erie. It seems quite clear that George Peacock's petition was turned down as he made a second petition, dated at Walpole on May 2, 1808. On this occasion he requested a Crown Lease of Lot 16, Front of Township, which amounts to most of what is now the cottage community of Peacock Point. There is no evidence to show that he was ever granted any land. In fact, there is overwhelming evidence to the contrary. A search in the Patent Office, Lands and Forests Department for the Province of Ontario discloses no allotment of land. Further to this, he and his son George Peacock Jr., were named by Major George C. Salmon of the second Norfolk Militia in return of persons in his beat who fled to the United States during the War of 1812. His son George Peacock Jr., also referred to as George Peacock the Younger, was also named in an inquisition taken at the Township of Charlotteville in the District of London on January 13th, 1818, and found to be in possession of no land.

Despite the fact that he was refused a lease of land, George Peacock stayed with his family in Walpole Township until the outset of the war of 1812. The authors of the Haldimand Norfolk Atlas of 1877 wrote that, "one of the first, if not the first white men who lived in Walpole was a man named Peacock from whom the point takes its name." They go on to say, "he did not, however, make any attempt at clearing a farm, but subsisted on fishing and shooting." They conclude their brief reference to him by stating, "he disappeared leaving no descendents to perpetuate his memory." At another point in the text they wrote, "a man named Peacock squatted on the end of the point of land which still bears his name. He lived by hunting and fishing and disappeared over fifty years ago."

It seems he must have squatted and "lived Indian" until on June 18, 1812, the United States of America declared war against Great Britain followed by an invasion of Canada. Along with many other ex-Americans, he and his family must have abandoned their home. Perhaps George Peacock and his family hid in the woods and made their way by land and water to Buffalo. This was certainly a prevalent occurrence as it was frequently noted in American newspapers of the time that people were making their way into the United States by any means possible including crossing the Niagara River on boats, flats, logs, rails, slabs and even without any buoy whatever, and further to this many crossed Lake Erie in winter according to the Buffalo Gazette of January 23, 1813, by walking across the ice.

In late 1812 and early 1813 the war was going badly for the British. On October 13th, 1812 they lost a great General when Isaac Brock was killed at the battle of Queenston Heights. In April of 1813 the American forces successfully invaded and captured the town of York. On September 9th of the same year the American naval commander O.H. Perry defeated the British and took sole possession of Lake Erie with the following words scribbled on the back of an old envelope, "We have met the enemy and they are ours." And shortly thereafter on October 5, the British were defeated at the Battle of Moraviantown where Tecumseh, the great Shawnee Chief, and brigadier General in charge of the Indian troops was killed. At this point in the war British General De Rottenburg ordered the disbanding of the militia and the abandonment of Upper Canada west of Kingston. The British regulars withdrew only as far as the property owned by Richard Beasley at Burlington Heights (now Hamilton) where they held fast under the leadership of General Vincent. This left most of the Niagara and London District open to plunder and the disaffected Canadians lost no time in taking advantage of the opportunity.

George Peacock and his son, George Peacock Jr. joined a band of marauders under the leadership disaffected Norfolk resident William Sutherland. According to the sworn statement of Simon Mabee, another member of the same band, they returned to Canada around October 9, 1813 and their object was to take public officers and public property. They engaged in raids along the Grand River and as far as Port Dover. Among those taken prisoner were Matthew Gilman, and William Francis both of whom were devoutly loyal to the British and both of whom occupied land very near to that refused to George Peacock several years earlier. According to John G. Harris, also a member of this band of raiders, the party consisted of upwards of forty men.

Alarmed by rumours concerning the marauders activities, and despite the fact that the local militia had been disbanded, upon two hours notice thirty six men met at he house of Port Dover resident Captain William Drake. They resolved to volunteer their services in defence of their homes and in doing so to set out immediately for the purpose of attacking and driving from their position any marauders that may be found. They chose Lieutenant-Colonel Henry Bostwick of the Norfolk militia to command the volunteers.

According to Colonel Bostwick's own account, "On the night of November 12th and early in the morning of the 13th, we pursued a band of marauders through the woods from the Grand River, and then along the lake to where we surprised them at the home of John Dunham. Mr. Dunham had made his home available on several occasions as a place of rendezvous. Captain John Bostwick took a small party and entered the house. He surprised them, but they soon took up their guns and commenced firing. We heard them from where we were outside the house and rushed to their assistance. After a brief exchange on both sides we subdued the traitors and took them prisoner."

This skirmish on November 13th, 1813, referred to locally as "The Battle of Nanticoke," resulted in George Peacock Jr. and several others being taken prisoner in possession of arms. The home of John Dunham was at the mouth of Nanticoke Creek in Walpole Township. One militia and three rebels lost their lives in the skirmish. The rebel dead are not identified. It is certainly possible and even likely that one of those killed there was George Peacock Sr., as he seems to have disappeared. George Peacock Jr. and the others captured were sent to the Grand River and from there taken by Indians to York gaol under the heavy guard where they were imprisoned in miserable and crowded conditions until May of 1814. At this time they were brought to stand trial in Ancaster, at the Court of Oyster, for the crime of High Treason.

The trial of George Peacock Jr. and the others who stood accused of High Treason has been called the Ancaster Bloody Assize, but was more officially known as the Court of Oyster and Terminer. The trial was held in the Union Hotel at Ancaster. It had been converted for the occasion from a hospital for the wounded from the Thames area. Here the prisoners, guarded, in leg irons and heavily manacled, were transported from the Union Mill where they were kept in a foul state in a deep hole under a trap door. The trial began with indictments on May 23, 1814. The trial of George Peacock Jr. in particular was held on the afternoon June 11, 1814 with Justice William Dummer Powell presiding, and John Beverly Robinson prosecuting. John Beverly Robinson was a mere twenty-three years old. He had been named attorney general of Upper Canada before he even graduated from law school. In fact at the time of the trial he had not yet earned his law degree. According to one fanciful account "he gazed across the crowded stuffy courtroom at the nineteen men who sat on a long rugged bench before him. Their hands were manacled and ponderous leg irons hung about their ankles. They had appeared here two weeks earlier to receive their indictment and a list of witnesses and jurors so that they could prepare a defence. On their faces the prosecutor could see regret, nervousness, fear, unconcern, and on some, scorn."

With a man by the name of Tenbrook as council for the defence, George Peacock Jr. was found guilty of High Treason. The witnesses for the crown were John Bostwick, Henry Bostwick, Jonathan Anstin, and Henry Medcalf, all present at the Battle of Nanticoke. The jury in the trial of George Peacock Jr. was comprised of prominent ultra-loyal New York State late-come loyalists of German descent such as John Horsinger and Philip Shaver, United Empire Loyalists such as John Bessy, John Smith, and Francis Goring, a man of great personal wealth and power and a large landowner in Niagara, and loyalist veterans of the Revolutionary war such as Butler's Ranger Benjamin Picard. Needless to say this was a "loaded" jury.

The court adjourned by proclamation for Wednesday, at Nine o'clock.

Of those tried, fourteen were convicted and one pleaded guilty. Chief Justice Scott pronounced the following sentence on June 21, 1814:

"Having been found guilty of the crime of High Treason you are to be taken to the place from whence you came and there to be drawn on hurdles to the place of execution where you are to be hanged by the neck but not until you are dead for you must be cut down alive and your entrails taken out and burnt before your faces (and your being still alive) then your heads to be cut off and your bodies divided into four quarters to be at the King's disposal. And God have mercy on your souls."

This was the only occasion of such sentence being pronounced on North American soil, and the last instance of its ever being declared in the Commonwealth. Isaiah Brink, Adam Crysler, John Dunham, Noah Payne Hopkins, Dayton Lindsey, George Peacock Jr., Benjamin Simmons, and Aaron Stevens were to suffer execution, seven of the original fifteen having been given clemency.

The grisly spectacle of the execution on a single gallows took place on Burlington Heights (Hamilton, Ontario) outside the military camp, on the west side of what was later to become Dundurn Street near its junction with York on July 20th, 1814. It was conducted by Sheriff Thomas Merritt of Niagara.

Contrary to the words expressed by the judge in passing sentence, the hangman tried to ensure that life was extinct before the victims were cut down and beheaded. As he must use a loose knot, however, the best the condemned could have hoped for was death by slow strangulation.

Small symbolic cuts were made in the bodies after they were cut down. This duty was most likely performed by the military surgeon (probably Surgeon General Muirhead) as Sheriff Thomas Merritt lacked the knowledge required to carry out the duty.

The heads were cut off and put on public display. The bodies were placed in caskets. The relatives of the traitors were given an opportunity to claim the bodies, though few did. The remaining caskets were then buried in a common grave on the site.

According to popular historian M.F. Campbell, writing of the execution in her book about the city of Hamilton, "It is said that Richard Beasley (justice of the peace for Barton) never fully recovered from the shock of the punishment meted out on his doorstep."

Accompanying the convicted traitors on the day of their execution was Christian Frederick Dencke, a Moravian missionary from the village of Fairfeild who had fled with his Indian congregation when the invading Americans burned their village. Brother Dencke had begun his ministrations to the prisoners on June 29 when the Government had requested his services for the condemned men. In his diary brother Dencke wrote that the criminals liked to have someone with them day and night to sing and pray.

"July 3, 1814, in the evening and on the following day...served for the traitors in Ancaster."

"July 18, 1814, went to the Burlington Heights to the traitors and came back after the execution on the 21st.

He remained with them constantly during their last days on earth and recalled them to penitence, and a reliance on the mercy of the crucified Redeemer. On their last day, as Brother Dencke repeated this verse to them, "they were launched into eternity and soon expired.

Jesu at my dissolution, take my longing soul to Thee;
Let They wounds at the conclusion of my life a refuge be;
When in death I close mine eyes, let me wake in Paradise;
In the endless bliss and glory, with the Saints of Heaven adore Thee.

"After they had been hanged," he wrote, "they were decapitated, put into coffins, and buried."

On July 20, 1814 there was a steady procession of rigs and pedestrians wending their way to the hanging, among them a sixteen year old boy who gave the following account as a reminiscence to a reporter on staff of the Hamilton Spectator:

"I was born in 1798, two miles from Hamilton...I saw eight men hanged the other side of Locke Street near Dundurn Castle. During the War they had given provisions to the enemy. A rude gallows had been erected with eight nooses. Four victims in each of two wagons were drawn under the gallows, the nooses adjusted, and then they drove the wagons off leaving the victims to strangle. Their contortions loosened the gallows so that a heavy brace came loose, fell and stuck one of the victims on the head, killing him instantly. Later their heads were chopped off and exhibited as traitors. Seven of them had been willing to die, but the eight pleaded for his life saying that he had done what he did out of a feeling of hospitality, and did not know whom he was entertaining. The execution was conducted by Sheriff Merritt of Niagara."

John Ryckman, an eye witness to the hanging
Hamilton Spectator, October 4, 1880

As for the land, in 1815 a man by the name of Henry Walker was granted Lease to Lot 16, Concession Front, the very land which constituted most of what is now Peacock Point. This is the same small parcel of land refused to George Peacock Sr. seven years before in May of 1808.

This Morning We Killed a Man, and this is How it Happened

John B. Lee

Today, this very morning, we killed Bob Dick and stole his horses. Damn good horses too. They was almost worth it. We come up the lake shore walkin' on the sand. It was about a mile from pa's old place and the sand was froze a little, which was quite strange for this early fall. Bob was still in bed so we was just going to take his horses and skedaddle. Trouble was Bob's hired man Jake Tooney was waitin' there with a loaded gun like he was expectin' us. I ain't absolutely too sure, but somebody must have tipped him to the fact that we was comin'. He didn't say nothin'. Just shot Tommy Martin in the ear. How a man can manage to make any kind of sound when his brains is hove in I don't know, but Tommy fell crowin' and whistlin' like a bird in a snake fight.

None of us knew he was dead till Jimmy Hyde screamed, "J-j-j-jesus H. C-c-c-christ. T-t-t-tommy's d-d-d-dead." And then we all seen the blood come leakin' out from under his head like rum from a busted rum jug.

Jake Tooney run in the house and we made quick for cover except John Dickson who never seemed afraid of nothin'. He just walked over to the barn, unlatched the door and in five minutes come out with two fine geldings of Bob Dick's bridled and ready to go.

We was all layin' low as dogs in the shade when Bob come racketing out onto the porch.

"You lead them horses back where you got them, Mister."

John Dickson just smiled. He has a way of smilin' that says the same as when other men split. I could see Pa out of the corner of my eye. He was lyin' very still, taking a bead on Robert Dick. It reminded me of how still Pa could be when he wanted to be. I'm pretty certain Pa was waitin' for some sign that Robert Dick was worth killin' when somebody else shot him right on the word Mister. Anyways, whoever it was made a mess of his face. He crashed back into the door and gargled blood for a whole minute before he expired. John

Dickson never stopped smilin'. He just turned around and walked away like he'd trick-traded for them horses. Pa eased the hammer of his piece and stutterin' Jimmy Hyde, he whimpered like he was a dog locked in a gutting shed.

We buried both corpses in the same grave. It looked a little like they was huddled together to keep out the cold. Funny thing about that business. They never tried any of us for the murder of Robert Dick. And both of them horses died from pneumonia. And I heard how Jake Tooney fell in the creek and drowned. When they found him he had a fish hook in both his eyes. My guess is, he must have been usin' the wrong kind of bait.

Before the Rattle

Crysler's Farm, November 11, 1813

Louisa Howerow

At almost dawn, the boy sucks on his fingers,
brings them back to life. He pinches his nose,

blows to clear it free. All night the razor sleet cut
through his jacket, britches. He curled cold-sodden

on the mud ground. Kindling and axed rails—the campfire
sputtered little warmth. Less so his moonless dream

of open graves, part must, part rot, and now forgotten.
He lifts the linen cover from his drum, pulls short

the ropes, the sliding leather ears, until the slackened
drum head's taut. The soldiers he's about to rouse

are coming round, bleary-eyed, cursing stiff backs,
ungiving limbs. The boy repairs to his appointed post,

shifts straight. The drum wears easier that way.
He holds his elbows high, the sticks above his eyes

and waits for distant taps. From right to left,
across the camps, each drummer boy picks up the call,

strikes hard. Feed horses, inspect the ammunition,
unlimber muskets, ram bayonets in place.

The drums' roll repeats, as one:
Ignore the ghosts' death-rattle. Reveille. Reveille.

The Night We Was Caught at John Dunham's

John B. Lee

The night we was caught at John Dunham's it all come crashin' down of a sudden. Everybody was talkin' big. Stutterin' Jimmy Hyde wasn't there. Neither was John Dickson. But there was about twenty or thirty of us good lads. One fella, Bartholomew Easton, have never come to one of these get togethers. And I wasn't too happy to have a newcomer in our midst on such an important night, but John Dunham, he vouched for his good faith, so I went along with it. I guess Bartholomew got his name on one of the disloyalty petitions and he was afraid they'd take his land too. There was bad blood between him and William Francis. Francis swore out a complaint against Easton's neighbour, cause he got to talkin' big, drunk talk, and then Easton got angry and so then he got to be a target too. Besides that, Easton's son got killed serving the militia under Francis, and Easton blamed Francis for his loss. So I guess he had a right to be there, but I wondered if we should be takin' in new blood just then.

Dayton Lindsay was there too. We was good friends and I guess both of us was tryin' to make the best of a bad situation. We was callin' Easton, "friend," layin' it on pretty thick. Sayin' how all his neighbours best get on side or they'd be lost after the Yanks won. And Easton, he weren't too sure he should be talkin' to anybody. But he was there that night, which is why he ain't in the world no more.

It was cold and wet and we could hear the rain lashin' at the little house tryin' to get in. I stepped out to relieve myself of Dunham's cheap rum. The door opened a crack, and Lindsay calls out to me, "George Jr...Get in here."

"What's up, Dayton?"

"Shhh. I thought I hear'd somethin'." He whispered so you could barely hear him above the fire cracklin' in the stone, and the rain hissing on the isinglass. Then I heard it too. A twig cracked somewhere's outside. I learned to listen like that when I was a boy, trappin' the line with my pa.

The air got sudden tight and close, like a smoky campfire goin' out wet under a cold kettle. I could smell the stink of fear in all twenty of them men. I seen Easton reach for his piece, which he kept loaded and set in the corner. My own musket was handy and I grabbed it and made quick and quiet work of the business I had to do. Easton was closest to the door when it swung open and in come two men I'd never clapped eyes on before. It was clear from the start they didn't mean us no good, and the one in front just seemed startled at first like as if it was his house and we was all there with our guns bristled up waitin' for a coon hunt.

"You're all under arrest." he said. His face all red and tight like he was constipated, his hair lashed down from the wet. Some of the boys set their pieces aside cause they thought that we was done for sure. But John, he just said there ain't but two of 'em and so everybody started pickin' up their guns again. That's when Bart Easton backed up and hit his butt on the table and the powder fired in that fella's face. Then all hell broke loose. Billy Smith, who weren't never too good with a fowling piece, he shot next and the ball went right through Bart Easton back to front. It come out carryin' his heartbeat with it.

We fired back and forth for a while, but it seemed that more of them boys just kept comin' till the shot was fallin' like hail in cabbage, and we was done for. I seen Billy Smith drop out by the fence. He was screamin' "I can't see, Jesus ma, I can't see." and crawlin' around like he was lookin' for somethin', then he just sagged down with his hands across his face, cryin' and clawin' at his eyes. Then he just went quiet. I don't know how many of us they got, but I saw one of their boys take a ball in the neck. I saw that cause it was me who'd put it there. He was a young lad, maybe twenty. He was rammin' his rod, and he looked right at me, saw it comin', his hands was shakin' like cock feathers when the ball went smack, and he went down on his knees and his hands shot up to his throat makin' a strangle sound as if dyin' was a game with rules to learn. It might have been funny if he hadn't looked so scared. His eyes was wide and wild. I could see he didn't quite believe what was happening to him til just that moment he couldn't catch his breath.

Things was real bad after that boy fell. We were surrounded. A few of us escaped down the lake. I don't know whether they got away clear or not. I heard later the brag that none of us got clear, but I still hope one or two did. I seen Pa sneak out through the woodpile, but it was dark, and things were flyin' thick and fast. Some boys said he was done for. Some says they heard he got away. Whatever the truth of it I never seen nor heard from him again, and it don't feel like he's in the world no more. I can't say exactly why. It just don't.

Dayton and me and about six others was trapped inside and we had either to give up or die in there. We was like foxes trapped in a nest with only but one way out and we could hear the hounds sniffin' at the hole. Dayton tore off a bit of Bart Easton's undershirt and tied it to his gun, broke John Dunham's window and that was the end of all the freedom I even knowed.

Them boys fast marched us out of there as if they thought we might get rescued or somethin', not knowin' that John Dickson was already down at Long Point, makin' a good landing. I hope the news got to him so he weren't too surprised when we missed him at the big show in Dover. The first fella, with the constipated face. He'd taken quite a powder burn out of Bart Easton's gun, and I suspect he'd bear the mark of that till he died.

The Whores Said

Keith Inman

Gilly learned about flight from the roof
of the livery, watching British Regulars
parade their paces, when his American cousin,
Abraham, started whistling stones at his head.
One grazed his shoulder and he mis-
stepped; bounced a foot in the dust.
Madam Lucielle called him Gilly with a limp.
He ended up in the ir-regulars learning
how to 'stick' a sack of grain, the townfolk
calling him Gimpy.
                                        Abe returned
in the summer talking about a Chesapeake
boarding and that Fulton's 'Nautilus' will sub-
marine any Brit-ship, "You jus' watch us."
And he jabbered on that ole Nap-o-lin
would never rule the world. Gilly's
third cousin, Holly, from upstate,
came too, coy and fair, all ribboned
and bowed in a New England flair.

Gil flew south into a new militia. A political
Captain, and his wall of other men's trophy's,
had a plan for Gil, and the re-making
of Newark. But he wasn't so lucky burning
his old home town, as the invaders re-
formed at the river. Some stray shot
tore his spine something good. Left him
with a double limp. By wars end, Holly

had flown toward fortunes in Quebec
and New Brunswick trade. The Neutrals helped Gil
flee across a bridge of buckled ice.

Back on the Upper, the only place that'd
serve him were the Whores, who'd watched
the Fort flare, and munitions red-rocket
glare through a Newark night. But,
a whole new line of capital flooded in.
He's a bit splintered of his own authority now,
throwin' his glass every then and again,
saying, he likes the way light flies.

Bootlegging

Keith Inman

Arms crossed against any whisper
of heat that scorched the corners
of Lillian's dark porch
racing flames had chased
the narrow town lanes
for sleeping Rangers who'd re-christened
Yankees with terror
Newark smoldered
in the wreckage of dawn.

And, the Bootleggers shack on the far
corner, an ash heap drowned
into ditches. The silent ambulance
of haloed horses steamed the air
with their breath.

Her steady stream of letters
poured into the wormed framework
of city hall; those
logger-headed men,
tasting her final straw
to their fiery existence. Though,
they'd pop-up anew,
days later, a month at most,
beyond some quilted huddle of farms.

Town folks picked through charred
timbers, their faces filled with shadows
of misfortune and silent prayer
for the dead.
And why, for heavens sake,
did their warring cousins
from across the river burn
a Bootlegger's on the other side of town.

Lillian rubbed lavender in her hands
and up her arms. She drew the curtains
and held her bible tight
against the flames that licked her rafters.

1814

SUPERIOR
CHIPPEWA
HUNTING GROUND
LAKE
HURON
LAKE MICHIGAN
LAKE ONTARIO
LAKE ERIE
LAKE SIMCOE
TEMISCAMING
N.W.C House
NIPISSING LAKE
Immense
Forest
POOTEWATOMES
MIAMIES
OOTEWAS
OOTAWAS
DETROIT
Norfolk
Suffolk
Essex
York
MIDLAND DISTRICT
CONNECTICUT RESERVE
O H I O
Pittsburg
Fᵗ Wayne
Fᵗ Adams
Fᵗ Recovery
Fᵗ Greenville
Fᵗ Jefferson
Fᵗ Joseph
Fᵗ Dearborn
Fᵗ Michilimakinac
Ohio River
Wabash R
Reference to the Townships in Canada
E A S T E R N D I S T R
M I D L A N D D I S T R
H O M E D I S T

Hand

Louisa Howerow

"My hand was taken up and a few boards nailed together for a coffin..."
—Shadrack Byfield, Private, 41st Foot, Black Rock, 1814

Would his Maker take a man who came to Him
Not whole? Lost limbs, he'd seen them

on the dung heap. His hand, too. Mercifully,
the dogs had not been at it. At night he finds

himself remembering the shock, warm blood,
staring at the wound, as if it were apart from him.

And just as quickly how pain had hammered
Through his arm, his hand. He'd asked not to be

held down, turned from the surgeon who stood
bespattered with another's pus and blood, turned

but couldn't block the sound—the saw blade
cutting flesh, scraping into splintered bone.

Silently, he damned it all, the war, the saw.
Later, rum and mulled wine helped, so did losing

thought itself, the way old men do.
His severed hand wanted but a little—

a snatch of prayer, a simple coffin, deep, deep hole.

Wounded By Bones

John B. Lee

I have seen men wounded by bones
the way a cannon ball
bowls the skull clean
in a sudden blink
and splintering off of the brain
so the body falls clear
and shouldered shorter for that decollation of battle
I have stood in the smoke
in the shattering air
with the shards of an arm
like the spearing off of a snapped branch
I have seen the musket's result
in the mingling failure of reach
when the injured hand's
like a bird
flexed with a hurt in the flesh too great to fly
fluxing its phalanges
and breaking the air as it falls on its fingers
playing the earth in octaves of stone
I have seen men
lean one way
on an empty tailor's last
the long gait gone into a cruel crawl and drag
and the useless
fluttering cuff ever after pinned on a fold
while a luckless
blindness comes flinting in the shaved glass

of a femur's second use
like whittled oak.
I have seen horses dropped
screaming red graze in a green mouth.
I have stood in the storm of war
in the terrible weather of guns
and seen half men blown by on the wind
in a crimson swath of fire and blood
and felt fear rise in the gorge
sick from the heat
where the heart heaves at the throat
like a hot apple swallowed whole and hard
and we have our reasons for this
valiant romancing of noise
all mad strangers
fools to quiet dying

writer, look along your paper path
regard the ghost of silence unsullied there
and who by what hammer, by what fuse
by what flint and wick
and tear of cloth
by what spark and pan
the vanishing comes to that small touch
the unwritten whispering away of the absent hand...

Picket Duty

Denis Robillard

6 PM
A bird, two birds
Three birds
Alighting on that silver branch
All is quiet, nothing to report.

9 PM
Darkness is slowly falling
I bundle up my jacket
Adjust my three cornered hat
My rifle to the shoulder and the ready
I ignore callouses
And the tedium of the mind
Nothing to report
But these savage noises
Jumping and staring from the perimeter
Of the fort.

11 PM
The big dipper is high in the sky
Spilling its star gruel into the vast unknown
Cold chill alights on those silver branches
Those birds are gone to sleep for the night.
Darkness envelops my soul
For another restless night,
I smell the scent of death.
There are no true words.
To spell out death.
Death is my report.

To Aid the Surgeon

Louisa Howerow

a requisitioned house, a barn, a tent—make do
a nurse, an orderly, if possible, preferably not slovenly or drunk

two basins
plus pewter bedpan, urinal

scale & weights

scalpels, curved needles
probes and forceps will extract bullets, teeth

trocar to puncture flesh, then drain

trephine to cut through the skull, reveal the pressure on the brain
                its spike holds blade in place

knives and saws for muscle, bone

speed is paramount

tourniquets advised, above the cut
leave flap of skin to wrap an exposed stump

rum, mulled wine
and for the others, strong men to hold them down

if non on hand
stout straps will do

Soldier Hospitalized at Niagara

Denis Robillard

This red-coat had slid by the sentinels
Made a foothold into my bloodstream
These turn coats over here are screaming
Telling them they won't find anything
Inside this fort but the smell of death
And the grotesque look of blackened flesh

I need a gentle sister to bathe these wounds
Don't give a damn what side she's on.
Send in Molly, she's take care of me, won't she?

I've lost something here in the dark.
This whiskey comfort amnesia just won't hold
anymore.

There's something trapped in my blood
Running amok like a crazy banshee
Maybe a Shawnee
is opening my gut up
Like a primed beaver carcass.

My blood churns like gruel
The trenches dug in deep
My fortification a helpless piece of skin and bones.
You can use my gnawed out nerves
Like guy wires and Rope walk your way
Across these lukocyted frozen rivers.

Gentle sister, before you leave these rounds
Shovel these nerve endings
Like it twas manure in a barn
Pile my blood heap upon heap upon heap.

Let my body rest here on this thin red line.
Another lost man in this battle for ground
And flayed flesh.

"Death is a Sleep that Has No Dreams"

Denis Robillard

Opening line of a poem attributed to Philip Freneau, poet of Revolution

At an unknown soldier's grave:

The shaman of the dark alphabet
Comes out to play on this hallowed ground
In this darkest hour while skeletons rise slowly
I morn for you
British
soldier
a man without a name
        who fought in the name
of Britain
Your un-signatured bones buried somewhere here
After an unfinished war.

I think of your bones, now fine dust
As the sabled wings of 9-11 carries us a decade further still.

Fall leaves
like red footed harbingers flitter about
Near this fort's entrance.
While a two century old ghost with torchlight vision
        peers luridly over my shoulders
        to quiz my approach.

All we have is our cold skin
These old bones
scattered in unmarked graves like yours
 Caked, muddy folded into the musty brown maps
of
 sand and forgotten time.

Your shadows linger
I too like a lingering bird
Will caw and kee and cree back
to this raven-haired trickster: death.

I will leave bread crumbs on the bed post
A saucer
of blood and milk on the mantle
To feed the dark animal that gnaws nightly at my dream brain.

Would it be prudent to stitch poems and Ophelia-like lines
Inside my red surged jacket now?

Will your roving dark brown eyes blast musket holes
And scatter my heart across this cursed Canadian landscape
As I try to leave?

In my mind is a piercing retort of gunfire
an endless feedback loops to your unfinished war.

The How of It

Ryerse Farm, May 15, 1814

Louisa Howerow

How quietly they came, how loudly
the dogs barked at the hills and fields

overrun with Yankee blue. How soldiers
barged in without a word, stumped past

the table, our bowls of barely eaten porridge,
to dig into the hearth. How Mother burst

from our home, a flurry of brown hem,
arms beating the morning air. How she stilled

at the officer's side, voice measured,
he listening, I growing smaller by the door,

my heart clenched. How easily flames seized timber,
and black smoke rose from barns and granary and

grist mill. Only the house and orchards stayed.
From that day, my mother stopped wishing

for her birthplace, planning to return. How we
heard no more stories of New York.

Vulture Of Paradise

James Deahl

From Burlington Heights I watch
a turkey vulture soar without one wingbeat
from Hamilton Harbour into Cootes Paradise.
There are people still living
who remember a time when
Cootes was solid rushes
a sweeping fresh water marsh before carp
cleaned out all vegetation.

Over a maple, hickory, and oak woodland,
northernmost home of the orchard oriole,
the vulture scans the forest's margin
for lunch: even the dead
have a role to play in Paradise. The summer
of 1814, eight men were drawn & quartered
where I stand. To the east the harbour opens,
to the west, another world.

The Going Out

Lake Champlain, Crab Island, September 11, 1814

Louisa Howerow

When the dead cross the lake in jolly boats,
they regret not wearing their going-out-best,

or having pocket change for the journey.
Coins unpaid, the ferryman lightens the load,

dumps the still warm entrails into the water,
They float alongside, enter the island's

rocky mouth. On shore, the dead ride on
crude biers past tents that won't hold moans

or startled shrieks, past clumps of poison ivy
to readied trenches. Here, they take time

to smoke, examine the hole's depth,
slant of its walls. The workmanship, they agree,

is slipshod, hurried. Nothing to be done, except
wrap their bodies in frayed blankets and descend.

Yank and Brit, face down, shoulder to shoulder,
squeeze in, make room for dismembered limbs.

Clods of earth hit their backs, fill up their ears,
the space between their throats and jutting chins.

Swain Corliss, Hero of Malcolm's Mills

Douglas Glover

(Now Oakland, Ontario),
November 1, 1814

In the morning, the men rubbed their eyes and saw Kentucky cavalry and Indians mounted on stolen farm horses cresting the hill on the opposite side of the valley. The Kentuckians looked weary and calm, their hollow eyes slitted with analyses. We were another problem to be solved; they had been solving problems all the way from Fort Detroit, mostly by killing, maiming and burning, which were the usual methods.

The Indians were Cherokee and Kickapoo, with some Muncies thrown in. They had eagle-feather rosettes and long hair down the sides of their heads and pain on their faces, which looked feminine in that light. Some wore scalps hanging at their belts.

They came over the hill in a column, silent as the steam rising from their mounts, and stopped to chew plug tobaccos or smoke clay pipes while they analyzed us. More Kentuckians coming on extended the line on either side of the track into the woods, dismounted and started to cook fires or fell asleep under their horses' bellies, with reins tied at the wrists.

General McArthur rode in with his staff, all dressed in blue, with brass buttons and dirty white facings. He spurred his mare to the front, where she shied and pranced and nearly fell on the steep downward incline. He gave a sign, and the Indians dismounted and walked down the road to push our pickets in. The Indians had an air of attending their eighty-seventh-or-so battle. They trudged down the dirt road bolt upright, with their muskets cradled, as though bored with the whole thing, as though they possessed some precise delineation of the zone of danger that bespoke a vast familiarity with death and dying.

The men who could count counted.

Somebody said, "Oh sweet Baby Jesus, if there's a one, there must be a thousand."

I should say that we had about four hundred—the 1st and 2nd Norfolk Militia, some Oxfords and Lincolns, six instructors from the 41st Foot and some local farmers who had come up the day before for the society.

Colonel Bostwick (the men called him Smiling Jack) stood higher up on the ridge behind our line, watching the enemy cross the valley with a spyglass, his red coat flapping at his thighs. He stood alone mostly. He had been shot in the leg at Frenchman's Creek and in the face at Nanticoke when he walked into the Dunham place and stumbled on Sutherland and Onstone's gang by accident. The wound on his face made him look as though he were smiling all the time, which was repellent and unnerved his troops in a fight.

Injun George, an old Chippeway who kept house in a hut above Troyer's Flats, was first up from the creek. He said he had seen a black snake in the water, which was bad luck. He said the Kickapoo had disappeared when he shot at them, which meant that they had learned the disappearing trick and had strong medicine. He himself had been trying to disappear for years with little success. Later, he shot a crow off the mill road, which he said was probably one of the Kickapoos.

A troop of Kentuckians came down the hill with ammunition pouches and Pennsylvania long rifles and started taking shots at McCall's company hiding behind a barricade of elm logs strung across the road. We could not reply much for lack of powder, so the Kentuckians stood out in the open on the stream back, smoking their white clay pipes and firing up at us. Others merely watched, or pissed down the hill, or washed their shirts and hung them out to dry, as though fighting and killing were just another domestic chore, like slopping pigs or putting up preserves.

Somebody said, "They are just like us except that we are not in Kentucky lifting scalps and stealing horses and trying to take over the place."

The balls sounded like pure-D evil thunking into the logs.

Someone else tried to raise a yell for King George, which fell flat, many men allowing as it was a mystery why King George had drawn his regulars across to the other side of the Grand River and burned the ferry scow so that they could not be here when the fighting started.

Thunk, thunk went the balls. A melancholy rain began to fall, running in muddy rivulets down the dirt track. Smoke from the Republican cook fires drifted down into the valley and hung over the mill race.

Colonel Bostwick caused some consternation coming down to be with his men, marching up and down just behind the line with that strange double grin on his face (his cheek tattooed with powder burns embedded in the skin) and an old officer's spontoon across his shoulders, exhorting us in a hoarse, excited mutter.

"Behold, ye infidels, ye armies of Gog and Magog, argents and familiars of Azazel. Smite, smite! O Lord, bless the children who go into battle in thy name. Remember, boys, the Hebrew kings did not scruple to saw their enemies with saw and harrow them with harrows of iron!"

Sergeant Major Collins of the 41st tried to make him lie down behind the snake fence, but the colonel shook him off, saying, "The men must see me." The sergeant took a spent ball in the forehead and went down. The ball bounced off, but he was dead nonetheless, a black knot sprouting between his browns like a third eye.

A sharpshooter with a good Pennsylvania Dutch long rifle can hit a man at three hundred yards, which is twice as far as any weapon we had could throw, let alone to be accurate. So far we had killed only one crow, which might or might not have been an enemy Indian.

Edwin Barton said, "I dreamt of Tamson Mabee all night. I threw her down in the hay last August, but she kept her hand over her hair pie and wouldn't let me. She ain't hardly fourteen. I'll bet I'm going to hell today."

Somebody said, "You ever done it with a squaw? A squaw'll lay quiet and not go all herky-jerky like a white woman. I prefer a squaw to a white woman any day."

And somebody else said, "I know a man over at Port Rowan who prefers hogs for the same reason."

This was war and whisky talking.

We lay in the rain, dreaming of wives and lovers, seeking amnesty in the hot purity of lust—yes, some furtively masturbating in the rain with cold hands. Across the valley, the Kentuckians seemed like creatures of the autumn and of rain, their amphibian eyes slitty with analysis. Our officers, Salmon and Ryerson, said we held good ground, whatever that meant, that the American army at Niagara was already moving back across the river that we had to stop McArthur from burning the mills of Norfolk so we could go on feeding King George's regulars.

Trapped in that valley, waiting for the demon cavalry to come whooping and shrieking across the swollen creak, we seemed to have entered some strange universe of curved space and strings of light. Rain fell in strings. Some of us were already dead, heroes of other wars and battles. We had been fighting since August 1812, when we went down the lake with Brock to the relief of Amherstburg. At times like these, we could foresee the mass extinction of the whole species, the world turned into a desert of glass.

Everything seemed familiar and inevitable. We had marched up from Culver's Tavern the day before. We had heard firing in the direction of Brant's Ford at duck, and awakened to see Kentucky cavalry and Indians emerging from the forest road and smoke rising from barn fires behind them. Evidently, given their history, Kentuckians are born to arson and mayhem. Now they sniped with passionate precision (thunk, thunk, went the balls), keeping us under cover while they moved troops down the steep bank.

Shielding our priming pans with our hats, we cursed the rain and passed the time calculating angles of assault. The mill pond, too deep except to swim, protected our left wing. That meant Salmon's boys would get hit first, thank goodness. Mrs. Malcolm and her Negro servant were busy moving trunks and armoires out of the house in case of fire. No one paid them any mind. All at once, we heard shouts and war cries deep in the woods downstream. Colonel Bostwick sent a scout, who returned a moment later to say McArthur's Indians had out-flanked us, crawling across a deadfall ford.

We stared at the clouds and saw fatherless youngsters weeping at the well, lonely widows sleeping with their hands tucked between their legs, and shadows moving with horrible wounds, arms or legs missing, brains dripping out their ears.

Someone said, "I can't stand this no more," stood up, and was shot in the spine, turning. He farted and lay on his face with his legs quivering. His legs shook like a snake with its back broken. The Kentuckians were throwing an amazing amount of hot lead our way.

The colonel smiled and shouted additional remarks against Azazel, then ordered McCall to stand at the elm-tree barricade while the rest retired. This was good news for us. We could get by without the mills of Norfolk; it was our bodies, our limbs, lungs, nerves and intestines we depended on for today and tomorrow.

McCall had Jo Kitchen, a noted pugilist, three of the Austin brothers, Edwin Barton and some others. We left them our powder and shot, which was ample for a few men. At the top of the valley, Swain Corliss turned back, cursing some of us who had begun to run. "Save your horse first, boys, and if you can, your women!" He was drunk. Many of us did not stop till we reached home, which is why they sometimes call this the Battle of the Foot Race.

Swain Corliss hailed from a family of violent Baptists with farms on the Boston Creek about three miles from Malcolm's. His brother Ashur had been wounded thirteen times in the war and had stood his ground at Lundy's Lane, which Swain had missed on account of ague. Swain did not much like his brother getting ahead of him like that.

He had a Brown Bess musket and a long-barreled dragoon pistol his father had bought broken from an officer. He turned at the top of the hill and started down into the racket of lead and Indian shouts. Musket balls swarmed round McCall's company like bees, some stinging. Swain took up a position against a tree, guarding the flank, and starting flinging lead back. Edwin Barton, shot through the thighs, loaded for him. Men kept getting up to leave, and Captain McCall would whack them over the shoulders with the flat of his sword.

Swain Corliss, pounding a rock into the barrel of his gun with a wooden mallet kept saying, "Boys, she may be rough, but she sure is regular."

Bees stung him.

That night, his father dreaming, dreamed a bee stung him in the throat and knew Swain Corliss was catching up to Ashur. He killed a Kentucky private coming over the creek on a cart horse. Then Swain Corliss shot the horse. Smoke emerged from the mill. Mrs. Malcolm ran around in a circle, fanning the smoke with a linen cloth. (Thunk, thunk, buzz, buzz went the balls.) Though we were running, we were with them. It was our boys fighting in the hollow. Colonel Bostwick sat on his race horse, Governor, at the top of the track.

The company gave ground, turning to fire every few yards. Martin Boughner tied a handkerchief to his ramrod and surrendered to an Indian. Swain Corliss tied up Edwin Barton's legs with his homespun shirt. Deaf from the guns, they had to shout.

"By the Jesus, Ned. I do believe it ain't hard to kill them when they stand around you like this."

"I mind a whore I knew in Chippawa-"

"Ned, I wished you'd stop bleeding so freely. I think they have kilt you."

"Yes."

They were in another place, a region of black light and maximum density. On the road, sweating with shame in the cold, we heard the muskets dwindle and go out. We saw Swain Corliss, white-faced, slumped against an oak amongst the dead smouldering leaves. Edwin's head in his lap, without a weapon except for his bayonet, which he held across his chest as Kickapoo warriors came up one by one, reverently touching Swain's shoulders with their musket barrels.

The Kentuckians had lost one dead, eight wounded and a couple of borrowed horses. That day, they burned the mill and one downstream and sent out patrols to catch stragglers, which they did, and then released after making them promise on the Good Book not to shoot at another person from the United States. The Indians skinned and butchered Edwin Barton's body, Ned having no further use for it.

During the night, three miles away, James Corliss dreamed that a venomous bee had stung him in the throat. Rising from his bed, he told the family, "Yonder, yer baby boy is dead or something." Then James Corliss went out into the darkness, hitched his horse to a stoneboat, placed a feather tick, pillows and sheets upon it, and started for the scene of the battle.

Prisoner of War

excerpt from *The Canadian Brothers*

Major John Richardson

Few situations in life are less enviable than that of the isolated prisoner of war. Far from the home of his affections, and compelled by the absence of all other companionship, to mix with those who, in manners, feelings, and national characteristics, form, as it were, a race apart from himself, his recollections, already sufficiently embittered by the depressing sense of captivity, are hourly awakened by some rude contrast wounding to his sensibilities, and even though no source of graver irritation should exist, a thousand petty annoyances, incident to the position, are magnified by chagrin from mole-hills into mountains. Such, however, would be the effect produced on one only, who, thrown by the accident of war into the situation of a captive, should have no grief more profound, no sorrow deeper seated than what arose from the being severed from old, and associated with new and undesired ties; one to whom life was full of the fairest buds of promise, and whose impatience of the present was only a burning desire to enter upon the future.

A Flame, a Burst of Light

Douglas Glover

Of the reasons for our lengthy and fatal sojourn in the swamps of Sandusky, there are several theories. 1) The Americans wished to exact vengeance for atrocities committed by Capt. Crawford's Indios on the Raisin River. 2) The Americans wished to prevent the men from rejoining their regiments before the close of the summer campaigns. 3) To supply the want of souls in the afterlife.

We were seven hundred dreamers starving and shivering to death in this gateway to the City of Dis.

Of the reasons for our deaths, there are no theories. Ague, fever (quartan, intermittent and acute) and the bloody flux carry us away. Old wounds, opened from damp and lack of common nutriment; pneumonia, dropsy, pthithis, galloping consumption, gangrene and suicide account for the rest. An alarming number of walking corpses attended the fallen like Swiss automatons in a magic show, then tottered off to expire face down in the bulrushes.

In the swamps of Sandusky, there were more corpses than souls. We had a surfeit of bodies. They were difficult to bury in the washing ooze.

Kingsland and Thompson, wraiths and daredevils, murderous on the day with the Springfields we borrowed from the Americans at Detroit, mounted amateur theatricals though much bothered at delivering their lines on a stage of sucking mud. Sgt. Collins, of Limerick and the 41st, took the female roles, warbling a sweet falsetto. I mind he scalped Kentuckians with his razor at the Battle of the Raisin, along with Tsenkwatawa's unspeakable Shawnee.

At Long Point in October, when we land, whale-boats and cutters rowed ashore by negro slaves with superior airs, a barefoot girl in a wedding dress skips down the cliff path after regimental medical wagons and surgeons on horseback. Over night, mist froze on the sails and sheets and shattered down on us like broken glass. We skate on the slick decks as the ships slide by the dunes and ponds along the point, mysterious and blood red from rotting sedge and fallen leaves.

The cliffs are dun-coloured clay banks undermined by the fall storms with great half-dead pines like ships' masts toppling down and thin cows and hobbled multi-coloured horses grazing on narrow zig-zag paths, low roofs and chimney smoke from a cluster of mean log and slab board houses above. We watch the girl, brown as a monkey, with ankles flashing beneath her dress, eyes wide at the sight of us. Preceding her, the medical wagons are like mastless ships with their iron kettles, great stirring spoons, and boxes of spirits and medicaments clanking listlessly. Clouds of geese and ducks, their wings flashing, lift and swirl over the point and settle again behind us.

I think of rhumb lines and wind roses and portolan charts. I imagine a map that indicates the vast populations of the dead, the departed souls like smoke spiraling up from the cemeteries, cities of corpses, suburbs of despair. The bodies of the newly dead make mournful humps of the sail cloth shroud spread over the deck. The boats roll and creak dolefully in the cold rain.

There are women among us, taken with the baggage at Moraviantown, who have lost all delicacy and shame due to the general deliquescence of bodies but yet display a pathetic dignity while voiding with the men or caring for their loved ones.

Except for a lucky few, we are all languid and ethereal, almost fleshless, pure soul, distilled by the elements and long-steeping first in the Camp Bull prison and then the Sandusky swamps by Lake Erie (shore-line of ill-fate). We all suffer the tormina and tenesmus associated with the flux. We gripe and strain and evacuate little balls or blood or pus and then evacuate again, thinking what a way to die.

Or we suffer the shivering chills, sweats and hallucinations of the ague.

Those who can lift their eyes to the gray cliffs and the medical wagons and mutter encouragement out of habit to the others. Some weep at the sight of the medical officers on exhausted horses plashing along the beach, squaddies at the double, without arms, hardbitten veterans of long campaigns in France and Spain and Canada. Music on top of the cliffs, dried up wild grape vines like nets or veins against the clay, exploding milkweed pods, and a spruced up boy in an over-size homespun tail-coat with clod-hopper boots, a red rag tied round his throat, loping down the track and jabbering to the brown girl in the wedding dress.

There is a girl in my boat dying, left behind by a husband in the Provincial Dragoons who went down at Sandusky before our fatally delayed departure, went down in the water, shaking himself to death and weeping in his girl's arms, terrified to die, cheeping for his mam, the girl overcome with adoration and embarrassment for him and running away to shit when her guts cramped so that she was away when he died and in despair—half-dead herself from despair—when she returned to find the camp grave-diggers already wrapping him in a canvas shroud they used over and over to preserve the dignities.

She is beside herself, shaking with the ague or shock, no pulse, almost a ghost, not a tear in her egg-like eyes, sunk in the dark socket of bone and lash.

As we are all beside ourselves, stumbling trinities of I and not-I and the world beyond that is like a curtain of sensation, all fluffs and billows like a linen sheet next to an open window in a gale.

We have the Americans to thank for enlisting us in an army of saints, yes, to thank for our education in asceticism and other-worldliness, for helping to disentangle our selves from the flesh as the desert hermits of old, our present state of dis-ease being a sign of something invisible that beckons.

In Sandusky, the energetic and the mad used their hands to dredge the swamp and construct islands for sleeping and standing and there was some attempt to keep up drilling in a shallow pond otherwise a home to bustards and ducks.

Sgt. Collins, always the wit, said, "I don't wish to die and go to Heaven. I have a fear of heights."

I report to Surgeon Kennedy of the 41st, whose dun stallion, name of Clarify, knocks me over in its prancing. Kennedy leaps down, striding along the sand, chewing a clay pipe with a goat and horns on the bowl, ordering fires built, the kettles on, stooping to speak to the prisoners, signing to his aides.

Already soldiers walk up and down with fresh apples and knives, offering slices to suck, rain falling the whole time, cold and dismal.

"Peruvian bark is wanted," I say, breathless at keeping up, teetering on my pins. "Charcoal and laudanum to bind the bowels and for pain. And blankets, man, blankets. Dry clothing. Clear soup with blood and plenty of water and salt, shreds of meat, not diced, pulped vegetables."

Surgeon Kennedy, saturnine, gloomy, sees the body as a flame, life as an explosion. He nods and nods and signs to his aides. He has a year at Edinburgh. I have no teaching at all but cut off a man's leg with a hatchet after the Raisin and sewed the flap with binder twine and, by God, he was strong enough to survive which was as good as a medical degree. The rest is bedside manner and prayer, I believe.

"Not five in fifty will see active service again," says Kennedy, measuring the ruined men.

"For God's sake, don't try to bleed anyone," I say. "They'll go off in a nonce."

"And who might you be?" he asks.

"Surgeon's Mate Netherby, Sir!" I say. "Of the 41st. I am a little altered condition, not up to scratch. I tried to save as many as I could—"

"God lord," says Surgeon Kennedy, a gleam of recognition under his scrutinizing brow.

"And brandy," I say. "I could do with a stiff toddy. Or something mulled, all hot with raw brown sugar, cloves and cinnamon. Have ye any cinnamon in the apothecary stores?"

"Go and lie down in the wagons," says Surgeon Kennedy.

The brown girl dashes from one only slightly animate bundle to another, dodging the skeletal perambulants who importune her with fatalistic courtesy.

"A mite to sup, Miss?—Have ye a hankee or a bit of rag for a blanket?—Hasty bint, ain't she? Always rushing about.—She's very clean. Never seen anything like it. Fancy she's just been to a wedding?"

Soldiers shake out blanket tents, anchoring them with bayonets, and one of the new style canvas round tents, snapping the cloth like cannon shots, strumming the guy ropes with their fingers. Fires blaze, fierce with snapping pitch, roofed with spits and sides of beef, night falling and the fires like the hecatombs of Greece glaring on the cliff face. Everything quiet and efficient. Quickly, quickly, for the dead are anxious along the shoreline where the Lake Erie waves slap indifferently.

The fiddle music has stopped. A line of villagers troops down the S-curve of the wagon track where rain water dashes in rivulets. Smell of meat roasting. The dragoon's wife lies in the sand wrapped in a officer's wool coat, her husband's busby, much trod upon and muddy, clasped in one thin, languorous hand. But for Sgt. Collins who attends her microscopically she would be dead already, has wanted to die.

Death has become an image of release from suffering. It beckons us all like a sultry lover, a whore in a basement cot, promising forgetfulness and release.

Her name is Edith, pronounced in the French way, Eh-deet. Her husband was a magistrate's son at York who enlisted in the dragoons because he could afford a horse and liked being above everyone else. But his death was violent, gross and humiliating. He was so full of bright life (a flame, an explosion). She loved the youth of him.

"I shall go to him," she said, quoting King David, "but he shall not return to me."

The brown girl falls to her knees in the wet sand next to dying soldier boy and begins to pray. Her bumpkin husband dabs at her hair with his red kerchief.

Sgt. Collins, heady with fever, leans down, his voice resolved to a hoarse croak. "Ye won't do him any good with that," he says.

"I am not afraid," she says to the tall, gaunt, black Irishman hanging over her.

"Ye should be," he says.

Then he says, "This one was from Cork, with a sweetheart named Red Brigid Delaney. He won't know the difference. Can ye be Red Brigid Delaney or are ye a useless whore?"

You can see her mull this over. On the one hand, prayer and everything she's ever been taught; on the other, the murderous transvestite Irishman, with his body courage and practical pity. No one has ever seemed as alive to her in that moment as Sgt. Collins.

"I can," she says with a steady look.

She has suddenly changed from the wild child skipping down the track in the rain, the near horizons of house yard and stump fence obliterated. Always the mystery of the boundless mercury-coloured lake and the local stories of witchery, seer stones and underwater monsters attracted her.

I remember the firing squads at Camp Bull along the Scioto where the river ran in reptilian loops by ancient mounds the provenance of which even the Indians have forgotten. Camp theories are divided as to their being raised by Egyptian or Phoenician travelers or whether they were remnants of once great indigenous civilizations now gone to dust.

Geography reminds us that each fevered and urgent moment of meaning will pass and that the wind of time is a cancer that destroys us all.

Four American deserters in dress uniforms, bottle green coats with black facings and shakos trimmed with braid standing at attention like tall green candles (explosions of light) with their backs to the lazy river and their coffins, painted black, open before them.

One man harangues his executioners, another sags at the knees then recovers, a chest heaves, puffs of smoke spit ragged down the line, the musket reports drift over the broken ground to the curious prisoners, the speaking man jerks, his shako topples neatly into the coffin. One man jumps up shrieking. The reserve squad steps forward smartly and shoots him again, yet he lies there still living, his body doing the herky-jerky til the blood is all out. The others rest quiet. Steam rises from their wounds. It is a chill morning. Mist rises from the river.

The next spring the freshets will drag the coffins out of their graves along the riverbank necessitating reburial.

At this stage, we have not begun to go off in great numbers. Our guards die as often as we do. Yet death is already an event of minor note, a mass execution being a dramatic occasion, a theatre of fatality, death as entertainment and diversion.

The camp hospital was at first chock full of the detritus of two lost battles, Erie and Moraviantown, though on the whole the wounds of the lake fight being the worst: bodies smashed under falling spars or loose cannons rolling along the deck, wounds filthy with shreds of sail or wood splinters, lads waiting patiently to get their bits cut off and then turning themselves out, like candles snuffing, equally patient, quiet as lambs.

It gives you vertigo to think. Everyone's life is a centre of a universe that evaporates at the moment of death.

But I do love a neat amputation.

And we bury our dead in the Indian mounds, mixing their bones with the bones of ancient men.

Sgt. Collins stumbles into Surgeon Kennedy, both reeking of spirits. Kennedy has stripped to his shirt in the rain to operate, every gesture spare and perfect and strong. His body a furnace, the damp steams off his shoulders. He pokes lint stoppers soaked in gin up his nostrils to combat the stink, steeps laudanum in a teapot, tipping the spout to his lips from time to time.

Collins wears his pantomime frock, burst at the waist, gray with filth.

Kennedy: "Sergeant, why are you dressed like that?"

Collins, reeling: "With permission, Sir. Not my colour, I know, Sir. There was a want of blue taffeta in the camps. Cruel treatment for a poor industrial weezer like me, Sir."

Kennedy: "Yer a bold squireen, Sergeant Collins."

Collins: "Nought can touch me now, yer honour, Sir."

They are old friends from fights on the Ohio shore and Moraviantown, when things went south for us, but Kennedy orders Field Punishment for the sake of form. Five strokes with his wrists bound to a medical wagon. Cut down, Collins drops on his knees, shakes himself like a dog, then staggers back to the sick looking refreshed, the flame inside burning fierce and hot.

At the Battle of the Raisin, Collins was on detached duty with Capt. Crawford's command, Shawnee savages dressed in scraps of stolen American uniforms, with Springfield and Kentucky rifles, hatchets and knives made of stone, sharper than razors. He conversed with the Tsenkwatawa and drank home brew whisky with the Potawatomi skin-changer

Crippled Hand, men whose style of bravery was mystical and unearthly cruel.

He was like Saul dancing among the prophets, and when he returned, he was not the same.

"I am not afraid," the girl says.

"You should be," says Collins, more strange than human, more alive than the rest of us. "I am conjoint with Death," he says.

The brown girl's boy dies at her breast. For an hour she commits adultery, becomes his lover, vows she will meet him in Paradise, kisses his cracked and infected lips, whispers dirty endearments in the shell of his ear where her tears catch, and presses his lank, algorific fingers between her legs to warm them.

She forgets herself in her pity, gives everything fiercely, a strange, grim joy in her heart.

She knows she has become a guide to the Land of the Dead. She knows the way.

Her present groom, centuries behind her in his naivete, looks sickly with the recognition of the unknowable risen up in the heart of his gamin lover. A pot roast man, clever with his hands, no imaginative throw, dull as a trivet.

She covers the boy's face with a blanket tail and turns to the next.

The first man she helps evacuate makes her gag, but she cleans him gently and thoughtfully, pouring hot water from a kettle, washing herself in the lake.

Sgt. Collins blows on a horn spoon of blood soup, picks out the solid bits with his fingers, and lifts Edith's head on his arm. Her thin blue lips refuse to open. But her eyes widen in fright. She does not want to be brought back.

"I shall go to him," she whispers.

The rain is turning to damp feathery snow flakes.

I limp past the horse lines, climb into a canvas topped wagon out of the rain, and nod off sharpish after wriggling into a sailcloth bag lying close to hand. Smell of sawdust and rotten meat in my nostrils, two coffins stacked on end, peaceful as a grave.

Wake up when they start to pile fresh corpses above me.

A drummer boy with a pencil and a list, look of terror on his face, says, "You b'aint dead."

I am paralyzed, wedged in, the wagon suddenly crowded with fatality. "I'm not dead," I say, testing the hypothesis. Corpses like cord wood on either side and on top, stiff and cold. I recognize old comrades, including Kingsland, the amateur thespian, hugging me in his bare blue arms, teeth bared in a snarl of rictus. The icy skin of a dead man is always a surprise.

"You were talking," he says. "I was sheltering and I heard voices in the dead wagon.

I thought the dead was talking."

"Can you get me out?" I say. "I'm really not dead."

"I told you," he says.

I crawl out of the dead wagon in time to watch great steaming drays lean into the incline as the first drafts of returning prisoners ferry up the cliff track and off on the road to Burlington where there is a real hospital.

There was another boy, just like this, shot for a deserter at Fort Bull. Out for a ramble, he got lost. A friendly innkeep said to stay the night and he'd vouch for him in the morning. But the innkeep hot-footed it to the camp and turned the boy in for the reward.

The firing squad wept, the boy awaited the sting of the musket balls with a look of weary disdain, disgusted with a world that had failed to live up to his expectations.

At the Battle of Lake Erie, we had farmers, distillers, printers, tanners, tailors, cobblers and carriage makers to sail the ships with the usual result. Moraviantown was a rout. We made a stand at the Thames but our hearts weren't in it because everyone knew we were only saving the General's coach and baggage. The Kentuckians marched up in waves and fired at thirty yards, mostly missing us, but we broke notwithstanding, the savages in the trees on our right fighting on gallantly to cover the retreat til Tecumseh fell, the last honourable man in British Canada by which I mean a fool.

Sgt. Collins and the one-day bride hover over Edith, the beach being depleted of all but the hopeless cases.

The girl's nipples stand out like walnuts in the rain.

Collins thrusts his hand into the fire. His eyes roll up white. Smell of burning hair. When he takes it out, it glows but is otherwise whole. Some parlor trick he learned from the wabeno warriors.

He says, "I'll be dead in a month. I have the sight."

Fires still blaze, souls blaze, the cliff face glimmers like the walls of a crypt under a ceiling of darkness. Whisps of mist drift in off the lake.

Surgeon Kennedy rests on a fish rack, tapping his clay pipe against his teeth, eyes smouldering with exhaustion and despair. Bodies not flames any more but skin bags, all the same on the inside, bone and gut and blood, fragile as a bubble. The face a thin mask of identity, the soul a hopeful mystery.

In his laudanum dreams he sees himself commanding the rearguard against Death and the intrepid Black Imps of Satan. But he's tired of fighting.

Edith bears herself in silence. You can see her thinking fiercely. There is much to remember, much to tally, going toward the Gate.

I shall go to him, she thinks, but he shall not return to me.

Sgt. Collins minds me watching, calls me, "Here, Lazarus," like a dog.

I think there's an earthquake but then notice I am trembling violently with ague. I note the telltale horripilation of the skin.

I am hallucinating, or the place seems tremendously holy. You can reach out a hand and touch the Other World.

A kindly apothecary's mate of the 41st, someone I once knew, wraps a blanket over my shoulders and bids me come closer to the fire. But I want to watch. I am already nostalgic for the yeasty richness of life, its sudden turns and dramas, its deep sadness, its mysterious and gorgeous purposelessness.

No one knows why Collins cares for Edith, but he is sudden and belligerent and understands by doing not thinking. He accepts what he cannot parse, doesn't mind that he will die, despises pain but doesn't fear it, and thus is completely at home in the world.

The girl from the cliff-top feeds him soup while he chaffes Edith's hand. She fears only that this moment will end, afraid she will be left to change her dress and become a wife. For her, too, action has leaped beyond what she can know. She thinks, All life is a quest for style.

An hour before daylight, a dreadful, somnolent calm falls upon the beach. Fires down to embers, the living, dead and dying blanketed lumps in the sand, one or two, still awake, stare at the fire.

The girl says, "It's my wedding night."

She pulls Collins down beside the jacent Edith.

Only one person has an eye to see, sleepless for fear he will sleep and die.

In the morning, a white rime of frost blankets the sleeping and the dead. The lake is still as ice.

Edith's skin is like the lake, translucent, blue and cold.

I shall go to him, she thinks.

Surgeon Kennedy presses her eyelids shut, thinking how she has attained invisibility (a flame, a burst of light) and a higher knowledge.

Sgt. Collins draws a uniform from stores, hangs it over his bones, whistles through his teeth hefting a new Springfield and a bayonet, tools of the trade. He is a man happy to have enemies, a regular Jonathan among the Philistines, and the Americans are so handy and numerous.

We blink, we wake up, we are in Canada, we are among the living.

It's not so much, state of anti-climax, chilly, damp, vexing people.

The sunlight over the lake is like milk.

In Sandusky, we were in the company of saints. We thought God was in the worms and maggots that ate the dead.

Smoke blasts from the horses' nostrils. Soldiers in red jackets (embers, flames) blow on their hands, kick sand over fires, piss against the cliff. The chinking of harness sounds cheerful and mundane.

The girl in the wedding dress takes a seat in the wounded wagon. Her face is pale, pinched, fierce and proud.

At the top of the track, as the wagons trundle through the village, the girl's husband strides along beside, waving his bandanna like a pennant, begging her to get down. But she doesn't answer, doesn't look.

Remnants of a wedding, slab tables in a stumpy field, clusters of wild asters in pots, a flag, a spit and a smoking ash pit.

She takes one final glance at the slate expanse of the lake, landscape of unease, imbrued with qualities that contradict reality.

At the last sorry log house, where a loyal Canadian pig roots in a garbage heap and another stands at the open front door, the husband stops and shies a rock at the departing column, face crimson with fury.

Five men of the 41st silently fall out, stack their muskets and chase him down among the houses, beating him unconscious with their fists.

Two weeks later, Sgt. Collins volunteers to go slaughter more Americans and dies (a tongue of flame, explosion of light) leading militia against the Kentucky cavalry at Malcolm's Mills. It is said the Canadians panicked and broke, leaving him on the field, where his body was much abused by Kickapoo scouts.

Of the girl, nothing else is known.

1815-16

SUPERIOR
CHIPPEWA HUNTING GROUND
LAKE HURON
LAKE ONTARIO
LAKE ERIE
LAKE SIMCOE
MIDLAND DISTRICT
CONNECTICUT RESERVE
POOTEWATOMES
MIAMIES
OTTAWAS
DETROIT
Pittsburg
Ohio River
Reference to the Townships in Canada
EASTERN DISTR
MIDLAND DISTR
HOME DISTR

The Battle of New Orleans—January 8, 1815

Gary E. Miller

The War of 1812: it was no more
than an addendum to a longer war,
a brushfire from a conflagration that
swept Europe, leapt the ocean, and then caught
in North America. But to the dead
or wounded, all who innocently bled,
who had houses or barns burned or their cattle
slaughtered to give strength to the troops for battle,
it was a major war.

At Queenston Heights
Sir Isaac Brock died; then more battle sites—
at Lundy's Lane, Stoney Creek, and Morav-
iantown where Tecumseh fell, twice brave,
until the last one in 1815,
where New Orleans was the most fitting scene.

The Mississippi, curving like a snake,
through rivers, swamps, and bayous, helped to make
the battleground a surrealistic chess-
board, a madman's jigsaw puzzle, a mess.
The British leaders moved their men and fell—
Pakenham, Gibbs, and Keane—the losses swell.
The shamed retreat was led by sir John Lambert,
who, (feeble gesture) to soothe the great hurt
to British pride, captured tiny fort Bowyer
and held it briefly. The war turned more sour.

For Andy Jackson, who successfully
defended New Orleans, this feat was the
first gambit in his campaign, an ascent
that made him seventh U.S. President.

Later, the news arrived: two weeks before,
in Ghent, a treaty hand ended the War.
Irony of ironies! A battle fought
after the War was over—all for nought.
Boundaries returned to pre-War ones and life
to normal for those who survived the strife.
A battle in a war unnecessary:
Who won? Who lost? Unanswerable query.

...He, who in concert with an earthly string...

William Wordsworth

... He, who in concert with an earthly string
Of Britain's acts would sing;
He with enraptured voice will tell
Of One whose spirit no reverse should quell;
Of One that 'mid the failing never failed—
Who paints how Britain struggled and prevailed
Shall represent her labouring with an eye
Of circumspect humanity;
Shall show her clothed with strength and skill,
All martial duties to fulfill;
In motion rapid as the lightning's gleam;
Fierce as the floodgate bursting at midnight
To rouse the wicked from their giddy dream—
Woe, woe to all that face her in the field!
Appalled she may not be, and cannot yield.

excerpt from part III of his poem commemorating the victory of England over Napoleon "The Morning of the Day Appointed for a General Thanksgiving, January 18, 1816

present day

SUPERIOR
CHIPPEWA HUNTING GROUND
LAKE HURON
LAKE ONTARIO
LAKE ERIE
POOTEWATOMES
OOTEWAS
MIAMIES
CONNECTICUT RESERVE
DETROIT
Immense Forest
LAKE TEMISCAMING
NIPISSING LAKE
OHIO
Pittsburg
Reference to the Townships in Canada
EASTERN DISTR
MIDLAND DISTR
HOME DISTR

From the Opposite Side of the Water

John B. Lee

What he met
from the North Sea coast —War
from over the English Channel —War
from over the Irish Sea —War
from the south shore of the lake —War
from the east bank of the green river —War
and then dying from war and going down
onto the dark and dreamless
ferry with his coin of purchase
the two brown pennies
of a new blindness
blinked into Charon's palm
and the calm still Styx
beneath them

From Europe to London —War
From Dublin to York —War
From Niagara through Black Rock
and beyond —War
From the great capitals of four nations
War—he fell on his bones
like a shocked branch
and was gone
let us cross over the river
and rest under the shade of the trees
let us go there
let us remove from the opposite
side of the water
let us make poems from fire

184

Billy Green's Horse

John B. Lee

What does it matter that Billy Green ran ...
the artist has sculpted him horsed.
And so
though history's hero
went racing shanks's' mare at the last
through the bush to the house on the hill
and so
though legend has it
that Levi lent Tip to the lad
as with hands
to withers of clay
Billy was mud-smoothed to his mount
under thumbs throbbing the mane
past Albion Mills
up the brow of the rock
to the camp on the Heights
above the blue bay.
But what does it grieve us
to think in the lag of the dark
he was lifted
by thunder or caught
like black cloth on a thorn
if we shrink to our facts
as with time
we are lied to
we're like hands to the hearts of the cold.

Smith's Knoll

James Deahl

The life of the dead is placed
in the memory of the living.
Cicero

It's from Manchester they came,
from Birmingham, from Sheffield
ploughboys released from their land
by the enclosures or
the unneeded children of the industrial poor
with nothing to do but starve.
With no plough to follow, no sheep to herd,
they followed their empty stomachs
across a land that no longer wanted them
into an urban dark that could not use them.
Eventually those who had not died
signed on to march for their Hanoverian King
in exchange for his promise
of a pound of meat and a loaf of bread per day.

So one day they marched into this
maple and elm wilderness on the edge
of a lake great as a sea,
and knew not where they were or why,
marching in wool on a hot June day
in a bath of sweat and mosquitoes.

Or they came from Kentucky or Virginia;
freckle-faced farm lads after adventure

or searching out a better future
in the territory north of the Great Lakes.
They found this field and pitched camp
by a creek with a wild rose border
almost ready to bloom, and the sweet scent
of flowering black locust spread over all.
For they were young men in the summer
of their lives, happy, perhaps,
as young men usually are to be alive
and on the move.

And yet they were surprised out of their lives
in the night of their sleep by the silent bayonet
or a hatchet releasing the brain's heartwood
from its dome of bone. Then the darkness was ablaze
with a confusion of musket fire so that
ploughboy clutched ploughboy
as they fell together into this anonymous spot
leaving their names behind, leaving
their pumping blood to sanctify this land ‹
the sons of Wiltshire and the sons
of the Blue Grass State
joined in Death's brotherhood.

All that was known to mothers
and sweethearts in England and America
was this: some returned from Upper Canada,
some did not.
And in the funeral earth
they lay these fleeting generations
without names or nations, unprayed for,
a jumble of marrowless bones

where wild roses are about to bloom
and robins call and the mosquitoes
winnow the summer air.

So we gather here this Sunday morning
one hundred and eighty-seven years
after American cannon fired from this knoll
to deliver, so prematurely, the souls
of young men to their maker.
Perhaps their soldiers' spirits see us now
as we stand ambiguous at their fresh grave:
Lieutenant Colonel Bob Barnes of the King's Regiment,
Major Simon Bailey, Royal Gloucestershire,
Berkshire, and Wiltshire Regiment,
Colonel Karen McClellan, United States Army,
Lieutenant Colonel Rick Mount Pleasant,
Canadian Forces ‹ and this poet, citizen
of the United States, yet loyal subject
of Queen Elizabeth II ‹and just perhaps
the dead can hear Last Post and Taps played
while the single wooden box of bones,
draped in the flags of two nations,
containing the only remains of
about twenty-one men,
is finally buried in consecrated ground.

As we pray their souls
towards heaven's peace,
we understand that we are as ambiguous
as these lost boys, who fell as enemies
to lie as brothers in their common coffin.
With our silent thoughts, and even our tears,

these soldiers of forgotten identity,
uncertain nationality, undocumented purpose
lie now and forever
in the wild rose shade.

Victoria Square

Bruce Meyer

The green bronze bust of a hatless soldier
looks bewildered on this January afternoon
as my daughter and I cross Victoria Square.

His round and awe-shot musket ball eyes
are loaded with the look of someone who lost
something proud and of great importance

but cannot remember what it was.
Rain on his epaulets falls like history.
The sky has swallowed our CN Tower.

I wanted to show my daughter the place
where pioneers were once remembered—
four hundred or more bodies—not a trace

among them left on stone; the peasants,
the founders, the defenders, the cursed,
lie beneath us like sleeping tenants

who occupy a basement flat. Katie, know
how your city runs on amnesia, the paths
and tunnels beneath the streets that show

no signs of the life below, places so worth
remembering that we keep them secret
and save them in stories and misplaced truth.

Think of the postcards I send of Torontos,
the pictures of buildings shining and bright,
of gold baked in bank tower windows

where we see blurred shadows of ourselves
imposed on Utopias and pristine under glass.
The square's soft earth sticks to our shoes.

The line between madness and hearty
genius is fine as the cables that stretch above,
stories crossing inside our heads, hung heavy

with tiny drops that falling fall and remain alone;
the tears I could cry if only I knew the depth
of the days we live, rain soaked, shivering for home.

Old Ironsides, Boston

late-summer, 2011

John B. Lee

we twenty grey Canadians
stood on the rain-soaked
decks of The Constitution
docked
in the navy yard
in Boston, we were
marveling at
the sky-drenched paint and polish
of the green rail bright with brass
and at the shining grain
of her Georgia live-oak hull
almost hearing the ghost-voice
"huzza—her sides are made
of iron ..."
those long-ago words
of the English sailor
impressed by how
the broadside cannonade
had bounced away like birdshot
and fallen
into Atlantic waters
plunging in
going deep
as the drowned afterthought
of a wave
curled under

but we
were touring the city
and this was a single stop

the pimple-faced boy ensign
offering
to answer
any questions—all questions

and I've one
I dare not ask

who wears
the blood mask
of that story

as he carries
the slow match
set burning
to the touch hole
of an ambergris sky
ragged with American weather
adrift
with gun smoke
from the cold smolder
of ceremonial re-enactment
and imaginary war

The Valiant Vacationist

Margaret Avison

When we started to climb those steps,
Stone steps up and echoing round and up,
I felt genteel enough, mistaking it for Brock's monument.

I don't remember why I knew
That woman we met (she was coming down)
Would never never never find the bottom.

Anyway, I knew at once
That this dutiful interlude would not be followed
By squashed-egg sandwiches and Coca-Cola.
Up till then we had never suspected
That there were any alternatives
To a picnic lunch in the park,
Beside the car, well away from the public toilets.

But here, on a halfway landing
An old fly guzzled a dirty windowpane:
I wanted to shake his hand or clap him on the shoulder
As my last countryman, and I could have cried
Because our hands were so far not the same
In size and shape and custom. And I knew
He didn't notice, and didn't even care.

After that landing came the wooden steps
With broken edges, and here and there
A crushed lily, a piece of old seaweed,

Smashed chalk of shells ground up with sawdust
And the naked air showing through—

And then, to the right, a river bank
Thin with young birches, where an old white horse
Grazed absently. The path led to the bridge
Slung over the sliding river's cloudy green
(Like an evening over your shoulder in early May)

Then the wooden steps again, and far below
The scrag and cliff. And then a morning pool
Misty, verging into the quicksand flats.

The word I send from here
Is pitched so fine it lances my tympanum
And I begin to wonder whether you hear it?

Moreover, last night's stars were plash
On my enamelled skull, and now I smell
The morgue-dawn will be snow, but myriad.

In the meantime anyway it might be wise
If I made arrangements only for myself
When I arrive. Then, if you come, we can surely
Find accommodation without any trouble.
I haven't met any tourists since last Sunday
Nor anyone else in fact.
Perhaps you'd better wait till you hear again.
Frost burns so quickly and the sun today
Was yellower than you are used to see it.
Their language here you wouldn't understand.
Myself, I find it difficult

and so far have been unsuccessful
  in finding anyone
        Even to interpret for me to myself.
When I have mastered it, I'll let you know.

Excerpt from "The Medicine Line"

Wallace Stegner

... It used to antagonize me, wondering whether or not the Canadians really did defeat the Americans at the Battle of Lundy's Lane during the War of 1812. It did not seem possible or likely, and yet there it was in the history book. Perhaps I reached the beginning of wisdom, of a sort, when I discovered Lundy's Lane, which loomed like Waterloo or Tours in the Canadian textbooks and in my anxious imagination, was dismissed as a frontier skirmish by histories written in the United States. The importance of the battle depended entirely on which side of the frontier you viewed it from.